Grimoires

Grimoires

The Sketch

Raymond J. Burt

authorHOUSE®

AuthorHouse™ UK Ltd.
1663 Liberty Drive
Bloomington, IN 47403   USA
www.authorhouse.co.uk
Phone: 0800.197.4150

Published by AuthorHouse 09/30/2013

ISBN: 978-1-4389-1725-2 (sc)

TABLE OF CONTENTS

THE MEET

He welled his eyes a fixated remembrance, of her, the glint eyelashes
The girl he would meet, fondly stared, the she welded her tail
She waited sadly, on the corner of Vine and Alowette
She wondered if this tall biker streak, would person her lovely heat
The tail winds blew hard that day, the autumn winds she blew
The bike shadowed a slide, another corner would come, a stare, a grimace
Before he would meet, the girl of his dreams, the leathers sweat,
A dry abundance of tears shed, the girl held her breath
A dark biker rounded the corner, of her street
She winced the perfume, of lady shay, she discreet
His were twilight, beckoning at odds, and the lamp-post
Beckoned, she drilled the autumn leaves flittered by the eerie foretell
She reconnoitered the hateful glance, the stiff lean, the prodigy of a child
She cried will your have mine to be your pet lover, for one night
As he pranced, the bike stood still, she wet the flicker, her eyes bled, red lips
Her sympathetic reasoning, her petty little hide away
They ne'er eloped, the park of Wallace, the deer found her mate

THE COVE

A Rock, a well of tears, the deepening wallows, the haven of porpoise
The wallow of the trench, the gutter, and the swimmers played
The haven of waters, pink, a purple, flayed, the green for depths
The mournful shadows, the shark's playground, steer of Deer-buffalo
The sword demarcation, the reef's permit, idol chatter
The bird's seaside bemusement, the idol gulls
They scatter the frolics of shadows, peaks, the wind rustles
The cruel hard depths, the seas collide, the dark patterns, shapes
On the horizon, the boats steer clear, the clear view solace
The dangerous view, the streamline adjustment, the rocky outline
The purples at sunset, the beige, the cruel baron currents
Mom once said steer clear the porpoise Rock, she caved the dwell
The dwelling of havens, still the Rocky, precipice hanged dangerously

SHARK BAY

The snapper point, the boats trailed a witness, the treachery
The inhibiting lone prey, the sharks, it swallowed boats whole
The shoals laid privy, the eloquence of barge
The fisheries, the stubborn shoals, they learched

The boats they cried-out, the loathsome warriors
Of the deep specter of the channel, the marker played
A bobbing St George's light charmed quietly in the distance
The menstrual curve, the buttress of iron the lowly light
The shark isle, it frightened, the grotesque images
The shark took a board, earlier on, the whalers fixed it
The snake haven of zero point, the depths of darkness quarreled
The spidery tale of snake haven, the bow creaked
The fiery myth, the shoals of hells, the limpet denial
The boats creaked, a salvo, a fighting thresher came aboard
The livers of fishermen, the giant wag-tailed frog it leaped
Another tall tale, as the shark bay, it cried-out

THE HUT 73

A Dyeline-caravan parks, a haven of shanty huts.
Rivers of lofty playful streams of tears
The nighttime vigil of kindly share the flounders
The snapper boats came home, the dregs of a lonely watch
The cat walks to the beginnings of Francis Jetty.
The long walk partakes, the feud tender
The scallop boats tied the moorings of whalers' pier.
They spillway the barge, fallen the drum of fin oil.
The skins market the seagulls fed
The local fisheries union sacked the fish.
The pardon of waves they lay a strait
They swabbed the decks, the flight of sails bled
The pillars of mercy Footing at pier of Port Arlington moors
The seaman's town. A folk lore of around the town.
A relative smite, the docks of prairie, sight unseen
A lazy bay of boats they sailed about the nectarine harbor

THE SILENT RUNNING

The gray-wolves, the steely sea-packs, the iron-bluff to port
The iron-monger, the battle 'ardened sailors
The steel wept, a subterfuge of under-sea combat
The reel worsened, the degree, the steely nerve
The combatants measured, the iron-horse, it capitates
The prop has loosed! The steely-eyed sailors, still
The Rembrandt of idol sherry, the skipper drank a squalid
The boson cried the ship has a bent nickel! The doe

The starboard clinker, the wet! He exclaimed

The submarine sunken other, the SS Harriers claimed, the torpedo

A periscope depth! The Captain whispered

The scope enlarged, the skip he ruse a tactile

The Texas-Oil! He whimpered, a charm

The stow the ballast, he whimpered

He crowed the periscope, the loss! The tub sunk

The Nazi onboard, the skeptic acquired

The Destroyer has blown! The Silent-Running Routine

THE SUB

The torpedo sharks the waters of grey wolves.

The tears of Allah they estrange the U boat, the destiny reeks.

The eloquence of fervor, the sea captain, a trident of usher.

He belts the whip, the china doll he ferments.

The liquor in the whiskey cabinet, a mule

He stows the crew he ravages hope, he crew the hatred.

The old patron the skipper of the overly old seethes.

He ushers a command he steals cesspool, the sub Bartholomew

The breadth a dark horse, the sea tiger down, He barks.

The straddle of enemy skins, the batteries ran dry

He provokes the steam, the bellies the trout.

The boilers they broke the bask of the rope, the violent seas

He cries the desolate of bongo straits, a graveyard of submarines

THE DEEP

The Jaques-Cousteu', the Rainbow Warrior

The sea enriches the greatest goods

The rasp of the mangoosa torrent, the Eel, he brandishes

The Moray-Eel, he stems the pool of dismay, the Shark he eddies

The floating, Man-of-War, the Starfish, he envelopes the tide

The Sea he belches, the tide of paint, the canvass of dreams

The starboard, the cantankerous bow

The Shell-fishes, the torrent, the dismay of oceans torrent

The spectacle driven, the seas, the violet coarse ways

The reefs, the array, the torn, mellowing capitulation

The elation, verdant, the tight man of Portuguese

The bask, the lady-of-bow, the rosy, the bow-waves delight

I fiend the generalization, the find, the treasures!

The Davey-Jones-Locker, I intrigue, the mellowing Cray!

The Locker and Coat, the Helium-Gas-Balloon
The stave the terrier, the save of my deep-sea
The suit I intrigue the butterflies the stolen oh the nitrogen philosophy!

THE LIONS OF THE SEA

The frontiers scorn of oceans parables of depth.
The watershed down, she burrows the slide
The mixed the druid of octopus. The weathering of snails permits a dry.
They rebuttal the curb a sing song old horse of spray
The woman cries them partial. The whaler toils gypsy ferments
The elapsed tide the start they blend, the oceans porous plankton thirst.
They lend them devout the silk worm, the vice of tears.
The Mendelssohn of worm he cries out.
The chatter of monks beneath, the ocean tide.

THE JET PILOT

A fighter he dreams, a waves of current, he flies
The staunch commando of the air, the waves, the jargon, the pigs with eyes
The intercom jerks, the squawk-box cries
The waver he slips and slides, the glide pattern
The slipping, the currents of the air, the plague of gender
The strongman, the Rio, his partner, he abuses the tenant struggle,
The under-belly, the forty-thousand leagues, the struggle, and the tail he whips
The gender of the cockpit whirls, the pilot struggles
The aircraft it hurls, a dawn sun run, he defeatist a smile
A nickel for the port-roll, the pardon, the skipper
Radio-call! It squawks the radar has a bogie on screen!
The porter laughs, the rollover complete!
The complacency gathered, the pew, he withered
The stock has a butterfly! The Rio laughed
The jet after-burners, the Richard, he crowed
The livestock has a bogie! The sights have a bogie
The butterfly launched, a paratrooper, he hurtled
A gathered smile, a Flame-out, he gathered
Hit the silk! The catapult has launched
A Vfive, has powered, the engines have exploded!
The silk, it burrowed deep, the pilot buried

THE FIGHTER

He flew the fighter, a curfew, the yield he plummet the wing.
A gossamer web the sight he enthralled, the fly by wire it flew.
The navigator he drowse. The map he read.
He flew the violet web, the hornet staggered, he trained his eyes.
The afterburners blazed a whine, the pull of gees, he cried
The nectarine of force it threw, the pocket of air he droned
The silver skies he fled, a drowned frog he bled

THE HORNET

The wire he flew the edge of the rainbow he wept.
He sunk a ship; the fighter blew the fires out, the winged hornet he plight
The shredded shorts plagued a rumor, he fired!
The missile flew the edge of the wire, he landed the aircraft carrier;
The winds blew, the updraught, a catastrophe he plummeted.
The craft swayed a Columbus of a virgin in flight.
The blight of oarsman fled, the nickel raged the edge
They steer a windage of joystick, the rudder flailed, the jeopardy of device carried,
A Prometheus splendor, the ploy he used the craft smiled, a saturated smile.
The Sagittarius ripped her wings, she preyed.
The savagery of jet it bemused, a starlit tempo.
The device landed the fuse beckoned, they brew the harmonics they still the wave.
A jet whimpers an oil of flameout, the drill, the courtesy of tempo.
The wipe of his brow, the covert of the rainbow.

THE SAILOR'S EPITAPH

The Baron-Seas he plummeted, he saw a vision, he drove the séance
He withered the snake, the pike arm he brewed the main-arm,
He scoured the wild seas, he broke the main stile, he cried
He weathered the sea; he broke the ship's mast, he scattered, the boiling seas,
He broke the coxswain, a call to the wild, the Wilson's point,
The jargon, the cat's eyes have seers, the weathered mast has plundered
The stroke of ketch, the hold is full of marble headed, the jackass drove the seer,
The port barrel has loosed, the Jack-rabbit he climbed, the tall-mast has jeered
The skipper he cried the tall-jeopardy, the seaman, he marveled,
He cried a Man-of-War has a pick-me-up!
He flew overboard, he scabbard the climb, the masts-men, threw a overcoat!

The lifebuoy he climbed, he built a scabbard, a recluse he stammered,
He cried if the buoy does hammer, the flotsam of Rescue plum,
The sinker he relieved the jargon

THE SAILOR

He dredged a colonel of sea salt, the whaler he broke
The sea he vehement, the tall sail.
His marsh the golden streak, the bow wave, the lady of silk.
The stem of tide, he carved his name, the mast he dreamt.
The pilot whale he stoked the Davy Jones Locker.
The lackey cried a broken mane, he silken the waves,
The old salt thrown overboard.
The boys caught the ketch, the hold he grabbed.
The terror of the waves, they drunkard the old swine,
A pitch and a whirl of the tide.
He gloated the sheepish grin, he drank a play' worth of sea salt.
The brown dog he sought the bull of the tide.
The chaplain said he sank brewers of salt water!
He climbed the sailors loop, a pardon prayed
The sickening peace he developed, the wallow he depraved
The pull of the depths he bullied a plea, he drove the broken Ketch.
The broken man of the seas he barged
Watchful blizzard! played a card, rummy shouted obscene!

THE TITANIC

The Titanic of steam, the boiler of refuge, the sea salts added
The decks she cried-out, the spring it seasoned
The old salt, the splurge of the tide, the season it dew,
The resplendent autumn breezes, the summery day
The upper class, they decked, the finery of the establishment
The poor they sweltered, below decks, the poor man's vintage
The cropper came, the silken wares, the abundance shattered
The iceberg came, a gripper he cried it struck!
The angry soiled napkin, the all will plunder, the seas have her!
The swift ordeal, the radio-man he scrawled SOS
His swift denial, to St Peter, he weathered the signal
The nearest ship, is yet to come, he sounded the bugle
He crept to the captain, he laughed, and the ship's distress is called
He maimed the rigors, the bottle of Johnny Walker'he drank
A red tailed whippet cried, the boilers are caput!

The sailors loaded the Jack knife, the spare boats, they have no more boats!
Load the upper class, the damned for the poor old ferry man!
He stowed the babies, he cried the Jack the coxswain
For the toads have been locked, the passage west, has a crewmember guarding the rest!
Seasons come, seasons fall, the sea took them all

THE STEAMER

The unsinkable of abroad, the titanic of steam.
The bastard of cookies memoirs, he strangled a blessed coxswain.
He fed the bow wave, the diverse honorary, servant.
They vilify that wave, the pure, and a draught of the shipping lanes.
They cry out the abundance of dwellings.
They 'bout the tortuous reef revelry of icecaps
The captain bredlow Smith, he larks the pride, the blue shipping title,
A Wentworth tug, he rasps the marvel of 'stead, a butler man servant.
The boats too few for a passenger of liddies extraction.
He dowses the swine of oceans' of pities reef.
The bulge he besiegers the stem, the beautiful relic
A trollop of sweet bread, he built the ships winery,
An architect, the winery of floozy, he permits the dragoon of steamship memory.
He flounders the port starboard, the fishes they sail the bow.
The wave of erectus sympathy, platter
They played the below decks, the organ of philanthropy

THE WIELDING ARROW

The Albert the Crossbow, he pierced the wind
He fired the Crossbow, he silken the fiber, he shot the monk
He calibrated the height, the distance, the trajectory
He sure-footed, the eye of the needle, he played the measure
The strength of the feather, he covered, the owl
He shot through the eye, the string it pierced
The owl followed, the flight of the bull
Spread firmly, the grip of the arrow
He pulled tight on the ring, the scurvy arrow died

THE BINDING ARROW

The arrow true, stay sharp, the binding arrow, it flies. Narrow straits.
The longbow cries, the steep it bulges, the crossbow, languishes a crime.

A proved narrow flight of old man buccaneer, the old man knight, his darkest plight.

The scabbard he brandishes the cower of sight, he grape burst,

The arrow pierces. the frond, the heart tears, the grape raptures,

As flight of the arrow, begets its target.

Too strait, too true sharp., too inebious, the arrowhead marks its target.

The blight of the corrupt the Wiley scourge of blight.

The thrust the arrow it whirls, winds a fish hook stare

The catapult it staggers, a tree marks its target

Blimey he caught the sharp end of the stick!

He begs the string the falconer's fright, the carnivore whips.

The bird of prey catches an arrow of flight.

The old fool he bends the bow.

He robes the old rasp, the wooden sling permits.

The bird it dives, thrust! A death of an arrow

THE FROGS IN THE MARSHES

The frog he leapt, he satire a pear, the marsh

He grabbed, the lily frond, he said the pond my spy!

The lily I make wise, the fern I grab, and I fulfill my destiny!

Grab the bleach, the near-side lily, I furnish

A bleak I despair, I rather would know!

The gleeful cherry, the spy I lay my riches, the despair

I cumquat, the qualities, I bereave, the tendencies reap

The fervor I long, the winged crevice, the mosquito

He livens the life, the tasty morsel grabs, the slippery tongue

The diva, my swallow of gaping horror

I believe I unexpected thee

I collide my sympathies of grape, the bubble burst

I succeed my gratitude member, the holocaust

My slippery gape, the fluid, I mistaken a vile

A love of beastly memoirs, I construe the Shepard

He plucked the greasy incubice, he harrowed the frog

THE SWAMP

The swampland lust approved the sling. The mud in the eye caught he.

He beckons; a slim tongue caches a fly of loop.

The bright eyed chipmunk catches the wasp, he whips the silver tongue.

The dye he flings, the parasite beckons.

The rampant frog litmus the triangle of death.

The lizard bites the old man frog. The sill of grimace wenches.

The bite it privies, the eloquence matters

THE WATER LILLIES

They splash and a ponder, the symphony of virgin lilies

The beauty squalor of willow, they pillage.

The marvel of frogs, they encourage, the bottlebrush of folly.

The winged needle of fernery, the playthings of nature's reserve

The garden eve sent to nurture, the grimace of delectable delight.

The ponds they splash, the inclement song, they bridle.

The back of sunlit pools, the splash of playthings

The reflection of chrysanthemum, they bloom.

The dusk of angelic, their forebears,

The imprudent layer of docile, the tadpoles.

The rivers flow the embarkation of cesspool.

The babe's tweedledum they refresh themselves.

The squalor, the tidal, the mosquito's rivet.

They lay the eggs of snatch, the grasp of the pockets, snout

The trout of summons graft, the rivers of delight.

The outlet, the swallows they march, the incandescent rock dwells.

The spiraling eddies do heed the scene, the swan Oh! So graceful!

Permit the heathen picker.

THE TRACK OF KOKODA

The digger of old, he walked the Kokoda

He construed the haven, he welled the fiercesome Japanese

He chased the yellow bastards, he cried shoot till dawn

He fired a dummy, he wept, and he shouldered the mate

He laughed, the stale Eddie, his mate the Doctor

He stayed the Rock-I-Ridge, the Burma Railroad

He scouted, the internment Camp, his mate the old digger

He flouted, the spoke, the Bonsai Warrior, he caused

The flatulent, the Japanese Cannibalized the food for scraps

He shot a black-eyed pea, the Japanese fought

The war of attrition, the wheel they grind, the Kokoda track, they delivered a sermon,

The Priest he racial the black, the soldiers they starving hungry, the bush, the outback

The Germans hid, the stolen booty, the Razorback Mountains

The scheme of things, the heathen Japanese, the starved

The dysentery bled them dry, the POW Camps, they fled

THE GUINEA HYLANDS

The diggers of old they rebuked the Japanese
The stealth fighters of jungle warfare
They board the destroyer of hospital ship, sunk.
The bilge they swallowed, the grim aftermath.
A sea salt pioneer, they broke the steed.
The wild buffalo, they begot the mule,
The Shepherd of the flock, the Clydesdale mule.
The bottlebrush they inhibit, swelter the mimic, the stolen they reap the harvest,
The old scallywags reaped the benefit, the Japanese, the bonsai of Ararat
The sword of blaze& glory, the festering wounds, the digger's blight
The thug they stole, the digger's blight
the dysentery, the caked hard boot, the blood stained clothes, the bacteria,
The lice of the bush, the malaria of mosquitoes they swarm the boots
The British talent for raising the English, flatulence.
The midget warrior of turmoil, the choking jungles of Rheumatism.
The panhandle gorge, the slosh of waves of Japanese.
The warriors that seed sleekest thou!
Strange pieces in a game of chess,
The dark eerie, foretell, the foe befallen thee
The appetite gesturing, the midsts, the stir of native hungry for food.
The tin of bully beef, the jerky tea, the liddies extraction.
The whimsical paradise, that be startles few, the bonsai charge, the sticky mud.
The parched bones of old jack, the desolate mustard pioneer.

THE MOUNT PLEASANT ROAD

A howling, twisting epitome, the shadows mirth
The trees darted-by, the heathen springs
The whip of the wheel, a strangulation run riled
A wild run, a purr of the accelerator,
The valves wrapped a wind rustled, a courteous chipmunk cried
A crier for the steering-arm, my pocket is heavy steered
The wild VC Valiant powered, the shrubs darted, alarmingly
The specter of trees, the wild marshlands of growth
The girls they huddled close together,
The man behind the wheel, he collided a tree,
The woodland premise seemed immense

PHEASANT CREEK

A twisting, winding road, a lover's lane he drove.
A spectacle of gravel coining the rabble.
A becoming of trees preached a sermon.
They diminished the subtle breezes.
The parable bleached the summerset.
The roses a deepening thrust.
The river bends, the blight of phantom-menace.
The wilds of track, the forests docile.
The burden, a mountain scrub, goat track.
He belt the whip, he cried the violet ferns.
The rivers discreet, by the wayside.
The member of the old lady, HK Utility.
The VC valiant he tweaked, the throttle.
The four wheeler drive, the tractor of ember flown.
The fires of campsite they bill the triangle.
A crescent butterfly, a witness.
The sling of rope, the romance of cow-dip.
The summer tide, the old Yarra River of bleak.
The summery day a skinny dip.
The paddle of canoes, they wet the hillside.
The shadows of fawn, the dew creek down.
The yarra creeks bend. The rile of laughing bathers they bask.

THE MONSALVAT

The heathen bout, the church lay about still
The Quasimodo, the dragon pooled
The depths enseason, the musketele, the weeping willows,
The hippies with baskets, weave the courteous grins
The pot smoking, grass sniffing pot pouri, the virgins at play, the birds they flaunt
The Arts and Crafts, a spectacular display, the museum of haven,
Antiphony of smiles, the playful aqueduct
The streams they play, the skinny-dip
The thatch hats, the polite gestures, the needle work
The flares, the stacker-boots, the mud brick work
The grub stew, the mud-brick cottages

NILLUMBIK

An olden church a hazy of days of old.
The romance of old, the cobblestone church.
The arts and crafts, the lofty hills they ordeal.
The hippies parade, the old bloke, they steal the zeal,
The omen of grass smoking hippie's paradise.
The Haven, they locust the pride, the Ovens Rivers run,
The local scene of Eltham shire, Town Park,
The pond of the golden lazy gorge.
The sour heather of Sea-grass ferments.
The yelp from local cattle dog, they suffer of a meal at supper time.
The local restaurateur, the Devonshire teas they sip the morning dew.

THE SAD EYES

Burning, saddest eyes, the silken loneliness
She appends, the rocks, the streams, have no-ending
Her lighter-lips, her casuarinas frolics
Her golden-locks, she 'bouts the audience of cockles
His brown-eyes, her satin bright, her eyes,
The silvery-glowing pores, the inlet, the grove of openings
Her liver of spontaneous, the gown she feathers
The cockles, oh shadowy myth!
She Delilah her heart-string, oh veritable lowliness
The sad eyes of cousin, the cat smooths the pathway
A tuft of hair, a silken, white dress
Her glowing smiles, cavalcade of tears, seethe I remorse, the salvo, the dress
The half-worn her ears, softly gathered
A fertile eloquence, a tongue speaks gaudiness
Her bide sweet-lower tongue, her voice
Be startled few, the resonance, the lovers voice, the prolonged
Her touch, she longs a remberence of you

A CHARM

A gleaming abundance of tears, mellow.
But why? How do those brilliant eyes, they soar!
Politely adding, the tears of locusts they do prey.
The puppy he adores, the possum of leniency.
The promise of hope, a gesture of hope
The dearest of darting sounds; a puppy laughs.

But why? Do you hound me, the torn remembrance of mine!
The bask the ambling furs distinct!
My distill the bequeathed tears, the torture of schemes, flatulent scenes.
So terrible the suffering, the plight of those ears they do prick.
An element of fear, a tear jerk, an adoring lifeless stare.

THE ROMANCE OF TEARS

The captivated wellness of tears.
The druid darkest hour, the beauty of passion leaves
They dispose the violet, the grub of silken negligee.
The curfew of pathway to the moon, shower of grief.
The pardon of leaves they floral, leave but nay.
But surely the hornet, the lice, the blessings privy.
The Excellency private the fig!
However, say not, the idol blessings of cumquat.
They delve not the shadows of primrose.
Do them not! The fig it expires, the lodgment of femaleness, aspires.
The lust of deep dark sorrows, pardon the primrose!
The deepening thrust they burden the lap,
The truss of weakling, and the shadows they leave a torment.
The true lust, they peruse the silken of arbitrary witness.
The idle betrothed the flower, a must cause, the deity foreshadowed the witness.
The rhyme he canst the diggers truss.
He feathers the blemish, the truth of allowances.
His creed of spread the witness, Gender!
They don't they muse thee pardon of grace, the girl she beckoned not.
He slithered hers, Pardon the tenacity!
The bruise he welcomed! The breakage of knee, he helped her.
The love deep-seated, anguish.

THE MOON SHONE

The Moon beamers shadowed, the forlorn sadness
The striking abundance of fur lined boots
The shadows, there's a grief, peculiar
The Boston Pops, the hungry little dwarf
Foreshadows! The partial, he leaves, the prominent Steptoe
The Jakin, Mister Jakin, his lakes a supreme, a craft he flies
The gentiles, they leave the crop-duster
The Hermes of Chariot, the web of dusk
The sped of craft, the litmus chamber

The helio he develops, he chases that missile, we must avoid, at all costs!
The daisy duke, the winged Prometheus
The spirit, the Slide-rule, he cries the onyx
The death-chamber he startles, he roams the quarter-deck, he cobwebs
The silver monument, down below a stow
His bleaks the no-nonsense, he cries Skipper
Streaks the no-nonsense, Mister Jakin

THE MOONBEAM

A meadows grin, she cried his impermanence.
She laughed the silly fashion of old time.
The jury she would face, her parents stagger, the crime.
They cauldron wet the child,
Put her in circumstance! A flatulent gesture.
But, how would, they know!
Would they approve, the fascist of politeness?
The beckoning, the shadowy stares, the other night.
At home, a dawn of mischief, a child they would have, bear
They might cause the scandal.
They may say, nay nor leave, the truth they may spill.
The trust of kisses of affection they shared.
The believers voice, to the contrary,
The motion, the boy into the cupboard.
He should wear the kisses of affection, the waxed pride, their son in law.
The trite beginnings, tradition of pride, the tradition of the Burt family sketch.
The tried and tested the olden times, they ask the old, the boy he helped.
The open minded parents they harshly wed.

THE KOKODA TRAIL

The Japanese hurled, the weights, the garden variety
The quill stayed sharp, the arrow found its mark
The dead lay still, awake the scuffle
The resolute suffering, the ham, he ate
The bully-beef, the strife wit the yellow bastards
They snoop the frigid allowance, the blemish, and the scar
The eyes do glint, the stow of freedom is upon us
The sneaky, he pries, he sledge a needle worth of salt
He declares, the country his open season
The barbarian, he paramount, the bonsai sword
A cut through the blind, the frogs they cry out

THE YOUNGER YEARS

The old Buick they shod, the old two seated, a court of dreams,
They played, a triumphant melody played the horrendous dew
They raced, the Dad and Dave of trivia, the dad and mum sold on the idea.
The trinkets of back seat motoring, they paddock bomb,
The taste of emphatic taste in denial, a sad remembrance,
The tractor, the track, the drives of old Harold and the misses
The old VC Valiant the driven of old, the boys' road the traffic island.
They chased the mimic, valiant of triumphant, the car they gave a merry chase.
The girl's flat they parked, a night of merriment.
The night was steady, a pot smoking, and bottles of bitter
A grub the bottle bled a thirst, Ian he lazy the sofa, a Perry martini he drank.
The music they marched on, the bottle coerced
The bat out of hell, Album! They grasped, the Queen! They scowled, the music played on.
They brook the tea they borrowed, an incense of scent, they futile a spell.
The billet the ocean flowered of lovemaking, the doze of sneakers, wet beds, a passion.
The dreams of consequence they drove a rambunctious evening.
The Dolan's picnic of constabulary, the Wet dreams,
The fish munroe he grabbed a girl, he cried drink to this party of tealeaf!
The idol chatters they laughed, they chastised the rugs of packrat.
The drunks had the whiskey under the table.
The brothel of Hydes parks, the city shopping guide to the west.
The tear they cried, the girl isn't the brightest!
They drove the Elwood beach, a day of frivolity, the Kitchener picnic, by the seaside.
They cradle the baby, out of the bath water.
The girls they playboy, played the music, the beanbags rampant the shoals.
The boys they saw a concert, the bat out of Hell tore the stage.
The ray' he broke the style, the stores he played the little girl of 19.
She grave the deep reverence to matters of indispence, the pity.
The number 13 tramway car to Elwood corner store, the derelict of Ararat,
The yea she remembered her pet boy', she starved the acquired kiss.
Of glory half witted slumbering boys she smiled

THE FIRST-LOVE

He laid the sofa, the girl he loved, her lovers arms strewn warmness,
The pact, the pet, her grandeur, she cried the bliss, a sweet young person,
A romance aspired, the tossed salad, the skirts
The breaking of hearts, they pampered the silk lining.
The strewn meadows, the still tears wept, the Greek eye shadow, the mascara flowed
They lay in bed, the stolen booty she shined, and her eyes dazzling his.

She showed his moustache, the work of tear, he beckoned her work, CJ Coles and co.

She cried to leave; he shadowed the tumultuous greens, the eyes beset hers

The sparkling eyes, she romanced the twain, they looked the stores of Queen's arcade.

Every step they took their footprints in the sand, the tenderness they stirred,

The simmer of growth, the forlorn rainbow, a requite.

The sparkling of reds, eyes of green, the others they redeemed

The qualities of petty mindedness, she suspected the tramp, the broken kiss.

The romance of simmer, that lasted years.

THE PET

An Angela of freedom, she boasts a colonel of glimmer.

A father of directorship, a business of belonging, the whiskey and coke,

The mansion of grace, the gardens rippon lea, oh so nice!

The fertile of spokes in a wheel of diplomacy, she loved the shining meadow,

The sheepish of Heraldry, the maiden she stout, the veritable madness

The fig variety, the garden variety princess, the greens of valleys pure of mice

The father he made her an angry bishop, a vicar she clamored the mice.

She cried for a mother, a moth beetle, she met his wind, the corner of anguish.

The vine they fell, the love they made, her passion of the Queen of Persia.

The purse she fabricated, a nurse of duty, a wallow of obscure, she purse her ladies tempo

The violet tears, the mouse she begged, a servant she be startled her passion,

A routine she strived, the house on the corner of strive and blemish

she hovered the stout, the biker streak, she wept the Angelis of bone & Clyde.

The embers of vine they borne, a fright, they kissed a melody.

The moment bestowed their grief, the pardon of lover, befit her allowance.

Mine gratification of deep morsels of passion, he wept her starlit vigil,

THE JENNY OF MELODY

She held a devout in policy to a husband of five boys,

A waver of the Glen, a warning found a polite no!

She must have written a boisterous note!

She up and left, the home she fled a nuisance, husband of thrice

She cordially welcomed a schizophrenic of depression.

A deepening laurels, a dowser, he bled the sixpenny dry, she wiped a hand,

A no! She exclaimed, the ocean of tears fed her dry,

A dove of dowser toil her happiness, she cried the boys over the drunkard.

She fled a husband of dry footed. a nuisance, ascribed her

He sixpenny a floozy, he fed the cumquat, the edge of the rainbow.

A pony strung her bad health, One threatened with a gun;

Shoot the in-laws in the head!

A dread of Wellness Rivers, of happiness,

A wake, an arbitrary colonist of the grade,

A bring home the wild two gun shoot, the afterwards of requisition of thanks giving

The Romeo of Hearts, tears he welled; the tears spread a thin nickel!

The pony, he loved, the boys he spread the envelope.

A pity the guilt spread thin, nickel, the hand of a womanizer

He blanket the wedded trivial, he rode the bedspread,

A copper-headed Romeo he spun the ridicule

THE TIARA OF GUILD

A happiness she girlish the pride, a show-girl she promenade

A silken of tempo, my meadows, her parents made a working-class-girl.

She laid the violet, a delight, a silver spoon of doughnuts.

She peddled, the grouse, of fashion, explicit denial

The kind of girl she is, she cried at the have not, from grace!

A symphony of curbed a space, she smiled a grape into submission.

A kindly Renoir of beginnings, no-nonsense spite will do!

Do Not waist my time!

A genuine of character flaw, lost the plot

I will not start by permitting a straw in my linen basket!

A thread of common decency, a flaw, she wept the tidy.

Her shed of impregnation of youth, sparkled.

The dread of euthanasia, a pocket of dime a dozen!

A strawberry of cantankerous, she bled the poor old diggers-routine-dry.

She found a gripe of single minded, potato shore a tear.

How I love the patch of silk-ripened-web!

The Martha a wedge tailed Ararat, they called, her petty allowances,

She spun a web, a needle of attraction,

Old Martha, her bouquet of rosary, she spun a squared, her heartache,

She blundered the right, she caught a blonde fellow,

She made his befit her allowance, an allowance from home, a pet-hate!

A Crete homeland she met a poor widow, she caught a flaw she laughed.

She prides her miniscule patron, to the studio.

THE FIEND

A personal care assistant, she cries a leadership of quarrel.

A duty of care, she met the door.

She person, my device, the person of Aids of wet nurse.

The nurse she prides herself. She frolics, the boys' of hers,

The pride, a rage of floral, she weeps, the boys, the ex convicts at heart

A spokesperson for the mob, she breaks a heart of torment,
For the street, she deluded a rival, she spent, a crying wilderness of silence
A medieval of garage sale of wench, she bargains the old time.
The tyrant of Canada, she riots, the Glenn of hostel.
The backpackers union, a spent rhythm, a bent nickel for silence.
A prince of men, a female of menopause, she gloats the sufferance of others.
The boss of the colonel, the bagman my hum,
He witch of the grade; a rampant idol.

THE LETTER FROM HOME

A letter from briar hill arrives, pardon the inevitable hope of ink to paper!
A girl he wrote, the spy, the end of a call, she smote the affection.
She brazed his little person, the ink it waited, and the tidal of inkling
The tiny little girl he dreamt, the beer he fought, he drunk a salt of peter
An affliction he buried, he billeted the angel, he raced the scribble.
The girl who sought a crazed, pen friend, a parent corrected, the dismal array,
She pardoned his indiscretion; she bought a rose of charm,
The wax of emblem on the paper, the papyrus of the violet,
The paper stayed, the ghostly Renoir she had painted.
Am I love yours, but only if it's to expectation!
The raspberry she anointed, she cried.
The cherry he blew, her emblem of fake tears, on paper.
She raved how the sparkle had left her, she colonial a spike a François of wine.
A cherry blossom hid the tear of eloquence, obscene
The spy she delved she cried, the moment they had left.
The pink fairy flower she upheaval, her tufts, a bosom she felt spite.
As the wave her hair drew closer, the fairy tale blossom.
The romance of the city lights gazed brightly.
Her need agreed his possum, the chipmunks they forfeiture the dismal;
A bird on the wire, the Romans of divinities, a sordid detail.
Aromas delectable, fathered the young, the spy she fell;

THE BLUE LIGHTENING

A silver streak proposed the girl, she arrived the noon bus from St Orleans.
The tramway cars they bustle, the noon day sun,
They golden butte, the funeral hearse he dabbled, the band sparkled
The silver streak laid a reef, they bludgeoned the treat,
The singing old ladies cried a voodoo spectacle, arisen the blues,
The fiber as the girl danced in the streets, she waxed a nightingale,
She peddled the shine on his boots.

The silver streak she hired, the motorcycle clamored,

The rider he plump her nipples, a witness she cried to stop me not!

The priest cloaked a hidden gentry, the rabbi crooked a mischief,

The corner of the band he hid,

He billed the rooster cried carve me not.

Yet, in disrepute the terms of endurance, the band played on,

The suffice endured a stiff nickel, the servants of slouch bled the cock.

They abode the streets, picked the reefers of salt.

The clan diverse in color, the Klux reviled the spectacle.

The award; they watched as they kissed the stupor;

Ground to a halt, the hearse stopped they bled the native soil.

The locals bled, the excitement surrendered,

The oceans of Orleans harbor, witnessed the spectacle

They plagued a thirst, the local boys had a won bar, they drunkard.

They bled a séance of trollop, the cried the drunker they gets

KATE

The girl, a Katrina of fiber length hair.

She laughed the motherly infatuation.

She drove a Plymouth dry of dry thirst, the local bar, aloud she cursed.

The rivers of fleas she pondered. The rivers of dreams, a title she succumbed.

She shared a little of her corkscrew antics, she fled the house.

A smile she damper, the held over republican ale. The boys they say so!

If they don't I'll liquor the snowman!

A defeatist of causes! She publicly announced.

A brook is as light a feather down quilt!

The boys of the house pardon the outspoken!

A Cartwright! She herded the cattle of Geoff the local boy

A romper stumper of vigilance, he denounce the doughnut,

Inhibited the crock of gander, i bet he dances better than he talks!

TAMARA

A bet you a mother has a crop duster!

The beetle antics of tiger, the red haired strawberry, blonde

She focused the mental addiction, a red haired focus.on coerce

The movies she likes that!

I move in a T shirt, a categorical in fashion!

The boyfriend thinks so! He does a good job!

He drives a beetle of gesture to goodness!

My heart is showing on my sleeve! The heart stammers quietly the cinemas

She slaved the cinemas, she bent the usher, down isle nine
The doorway of ceremony, her lethargy the silver screen.
A park royal, the house, a couth the wild strawberry
I'd better keep the clients at heart, the better side of the stroke!
They cry my need they boast a quiet of allsorts!
The ocean of rugs, the laundry must can do!
His carriageway the possum of Geoff, he smiles my undergarment.
The mc Minn clan, the father he mimics.
His hypothesis the rogue, the brave man of the diggers!
The clientele they spoke loudly they don't understand the cloth.
The shrill of defeatist struggle, the grape, I can't drink!
The red haired old lady, the uniform they docile!
They dream the sponge of wedlock; The Maureen a lucky doll!
The Katrina she rules the waves, I do not!

THE ROUGHNECKS

The boys of the rig they alighted the tower.
The fuse broke the stem of gas pipeline.
They bled the pompous old Harry stumper, his gas of old red dog
The wine of forbidden, he built the oil rigger, he broke the relief valve,
And the stem shot the mount, old molly the mount
She spout the tube through the center of the gap.
The oil flew the aloof the roof, the cushion of red salt
The valves they flew through the needle, they jumped at old Pegasus the wheel man
He blew the screw; he sunk the tub, the rigors they havoc the strongarm blight
The pike smothered the wheel house, the blight of gas pocket.
It screwed the plight, and it dug in, a scramble for the mess
The AJ he smote the two-legged variety, the bosses daughter, he smug
He took the tube the seamen's old rubber nickel

THE STOWAWAY

He stowed the sour kraut and cheese, he hid the bottom of the cabin.
The lifeboat he hid the sailors oars, the boats they cabin he stowed.
The lather of fish eyed jacks they rake a smitten
The effortless they move they find the cabin boy stranded.
The pickle the jar, the Ivan of scabbard, shackle him to the rails!
The skipper he dodges, whimper of oil soaked rags
The thirst they pillage, the old cabin boy rallied, the boys whipped him.
The lifeboats of rigors, the turtle they called old yellow!
The fruits have stayed, the rampant the pig they Zoë the arch deacon

The boy of hutch grew a haven of common bitter salts
The cabin boy' stuck the fruit pie the lemon he chewed
They salute the barge, the frigate of the open seas
The stowaway he grouse, the sour kraut
He poked a boil, the whalers of dream they smite a Mornington straits
Away o' away the boys sung the oars have a pledge!
The load for a cabin boy they strayed, a sixpence
The pinkie stayed she's a whaler without a cabin boy!
They pickled the rum rations; they steal the oceans of cleft.

THE BABY BOOMERS

They created havoc austere of flat nosed dolphin
They grimy eyed they went the parties of Woodstock
They revolution an era of Rock and Roll.
The lost survivors of forgotten generation.
They stole the hats, an umbrella of tidy old Scottish pride.
They enveloped a chaperone, the older set they regardless the set
They wore flares the shogun of footstep boots.
The collar and tie, the speakeasy of wellness, the polythene rain coats.
The dinner of rebuke, the concerts they plagued a ripe.
The sea grass they hid a smile.
The orchestra of Glenn Miller a downer of outer.
The movement of popular music, they fruit the gay-sectarian violence
The oceans of tide, the Bob a stylized hunchback of pop
A country and western, the idol of the big O!
He brought the sport, the trivia of Woodstock

THE BOTTLEBRUSH

The bottlebrush lives Tightly-woven the proliferation of virtue.
The stems they arisen the tide, the foul they say!
The wooded Prometheus of enormous whaler!
At odds they spelt the pollen of the insect, he befuddles,
The wed they say, a bottlebrush of timber, a virgin of twilight,
The wolves they do prey, they mask the facade deeply in the night!
They open the embers of night, the sky a threaded falcon of disbelief
Do they havoc the cherry of bottle nosed floral the haven of cherries
The facade the spiraling of evident, the native they do spell the spoils
A wicked of cherry, the wild of elegance, the rage violets, they plague the bitter swirls
The prey of hard gum nuts they spray the wild, the catapults of nectar,
The arrows of seed the mule hard to crack!

The nuts they fly open, the rivers of gold a must can do!
They pride themselves, the baron species of turtle necked lizards,
They, the embers fly above, the smoke, the fires prey the silken embers.

NAOMI

A classic aware with five kids, and two girls of the younger set.
A barrel full of laughs a single of a mind, to be, an expressive of youth.
An independent three boys, a sour of Clydesdale a hearsay!
You can't be my mouth of frontiers, the stroke of luck.
The taxis broke, a astound of perilous they drove
A needle of infatuation prepared a married for the time.
The Paul, a Bonaparte of wedded bliss, a clown
A Murphy of wild the cantankerous Paul, he speed the cab
A sociable of mixed affairs to begin with, he dowses the River Phoenix
He broke the van, a sociopath of a scoundrel.
She loves the hairline of Frigidaire a magnet for the meadows stare.
He grim the shuttle a bus of rain dog's back.down a furlined seat
The spelt the fur of reckless ambition, a mechanic of the grade.
A Naomi a classic frontier, a laxity of ways, she cries her kids, they yell
The hammer down they cry, the steely eyed midget on a phone

KING PARROT CREEK

The whole family packed the bags, a scallywag he fought
The strawberry patch of Ackeron valley heights.
They rebuttal of nerve, the mount slide of picnic ground.
The hollow of sleepy midst, the wallow, the pardon the pair, the crickets they do tell a tale.
The prairie of waste, the awaited the grim silence of servitude, apt
The Walter and Ken, a Harold finicky pair, the wooded frontier.
The kids of spectacle, they cried, ask me how!
They cried the parrot where is the cherry!
The gloat of grandpa, he clientele the whicker, the dry pan of dirt. shovel of Petri
The bush shovel for the licorice bandit, the toilet in the woods.
They prolific the bundle, the shooters they cried, a wonder of spoils!
The rabbit in the growth, a lair, a spurn on the sheepish grin.
The fathers taken a potshot, a Slazenger 22 rim fire he despaired a drink
He hit the egg of spoils, the son of reviled an evident view a mischief narrowed the bullock
He fought the cattle crossing, the bridge of imminent stead, the paddock he rascal

THE SCAPE

A wonderland view, the Isosceles-creek triangle.
Pardon the bush, the block of wooded tree ferns, of lazy days.
The Eildon of old Toms' cabin, he spoke of the fires.
The rage of furnace the dwellings, he burnt, the fiery of rage
The cabin it burnt to the ground, old Goldie suffered
The frontiers, the birdlife of lyrebirds, the peacock angry at the smidgens.
The toil of sugarloaf, the mount, it hovered discreetly in the midst.
The tree that lived before Christendom times.
The chickens an easy prey, say the sledge of the wellness of Sweet-bread
The cockneys breasted, he chook the shoot
The rooted, a spring of water, deep the caverns,
The catacombs of ravines playful, the waterfall they played.
The beautiful scenic of Arthur's creek.
The bend the Dwight's falls, the locusts, the hornet frog.
The toad the spring butterfly, the imp of stony eyed caterpillar
The cabin burnt to the ground, Old Goldie sank the rabbit! Hearsay!
He built a cline of thrust, the angry mule down the slopes of frontier isle.

MARIE

A cannery of SPC she works, a labor of love', she works
A pleasant of the Galway she is driven a courtesy of Brickworks
The home a wicked pantry, the homely she cold a slather of the beetle,
She cries her children, a loan to bury her sympathies
A nicety of glamour, a loathsome of patronage.
She weeps for the husband, she says the work is an adult of many privy mercies!
She broke the style, she clavicle the brewers ale, the mice they carry me!
I am a woeful of contrite, a meadow fields of glory, and a stray cook!
Paul! He meets the bundle of merciful of sweet abundance of amenity.
A dowser of food for the nickel, a restaurateur she paddocks her tender mercies.
She weeps the clientele, the stream of sweet mercies
She cries the morsel of gradual beginnings, a tried the hardest I could!
In vain. The parental consent to a Devonshire potato.
The evident pride, the worshipful of blessings.
The petty, dressing table. The mouthful of lipstick, Mermaid of sweet perfume.
Sweet vermouth after the work, for a patronage of Galway's!
My kindness lives bequeath the kindness she sheds

LIBBY

A librarian of sympathies, she melted a pride of others
Her hemlock the humdinger of pride.
A pride of worship, she cried the phosphor lamp, into the corner
A straight talker she infernal the draft, acquired synthesis, she spoke.
She grew up in the time of hippies.
She laughed the Cossacks of fame, a bright eyed lassie.
She cried the drugs, the gangs she loathed
He peddles a book of poetry I love, the clavicle I loath
The slight retiring gesture of clavicle, a book of a 1000 words.
A root into the cause of inner self, the immortal of guide into gentle
A genuine she belittle the author, the prowess the honeysuckle
A remote of gesturing she steers, the farm, a curdle of worship
The they loved her feat of merriment, she defeatist none
She cried a dwarf of shrubbery, she noticed the verb.
The papers held her amused, a Shakespearean epic of grim notoriety.
The old time epic gesturing of elementary

DARNIE

Silken dew, a nectarine of apple, a child of the poor
She wed a husband a fertile abandonment, she caught the lover online
She cried the lover on-screen she flirted, a youngster of 14 she wept.
She hovered a sweet mercy, a pride of buttercup, and the elusive devy.
A halt she demanded, the many fine mercies she found.hope
The son a Motor-cross rider, she spent a bullion of pesos,
She docile a want not, she cried with anguish, he finished school.
A teacher she wanted, her mother wept, a methodical strain, a purpose for life,
A gang he rampant, a silver spoon of methodical twin,
A colloquial now and then, I like to ride the trails
He pardoned the hope liquor by trade.
He swung the devy sung a golden voice.
A Hip Hop she cried, a boy 'cried no such thing!
She worried the internet, a substance she found a willingness to succeed.
She bought a load, buttered bread, a low the cup of milk she pampered.
She loves of mother a baby niece; she croaked the splendor of adulthood.
The uncle laugh a lot she defamed, a sweet kiss, she asked an I-pod.
She laments a fashion of a baby girl,
She laments the Australian into a corner.

LISA

She was spokesperson for the mob; she spoke as dirty Russell, the potter.

The ex con, she lather a spout, the tyrant she roamed a device.

She led a trail of glimmer a spout for a bottle of sweenies ointment.

She laments a drunk, a shallow decadence she cried.

The bottle shop she drank, the boys of town she peddled a bottle.

A tramp she spoiled a street kid's flagon of port.

A nestle with a boy, a feud of sweet perfume.

Guitar music! She strum, she borrowed the townie.

The old Belvedere, the street drunkard, and a murderer she defamed.

The Alfred of swine, the tankard of grass roots,

The bottle she claimed her very own

THE HUSTLER

A Street beckoned the ladies of the night, firm, stout the brewers nectar

The sour of the dark, the walkers of the stretch, the leathers tight

The palladium of St Kilda, the city lights, the gazes of onlookers.

The strewn shallow decadence, the strewn eye shadow, the mascara flowed

The lush city streets, the hive of activity, the windows, the pimps cold stares of blank

The Riverina of hush, the church steeple a brothel, the contemptful swine.

The ladies of the night, the pearl negligee, the hive of worms.

The Lansdowne Street, her crime of petty, the police they laughed.

The brothel of incarnate, the teens they peddled their bodies.

The hush of sneakers, play of pimps, sworn elope of trades they scurried

THE SPIDER AND THE FLY

The professor he league a court of the spider.

He invented a machine, transpose the violet.into a dimension

A machine the fiber, the spider cornered a palace of dreams

A transpose of liqueur, the new location, and the palace he flew.

A new place in time, a Harriet he wasp,

Was the blend, he placed himself!

He transposed the myth, he chased the lady,

And he wanted a Jekyll and Hyde into a chamber.

He groped the spider alleviated spite, the chamber he surmised.

The electrocardiograph the tumultuous guinea pig

The spider an egg, it caricatured the bright of colossus.

The whining, the lights on and off, the stem implant he lit, and fly

A fly landed the transpose of nickel bled; a machine lit the well oiled widget

The bulbs they flashed the neutrons they cried.

A loud humming, the fly had cache, the fixed element of farce.

The machine rattled a patriot doomed, the scientist cried.

He had become a fly in a bottle, a flea of Simmons ointment

THE STRANDED K 17

The sub it laughed a stray of founder it blew.

The steel of the hull erupted a keel.shattered

The reactor core sandwiched the element, a molten valve pierced the brook

The slum of the depths, the oceans they pardon assault.

The deadly ravaged the slime of bodies, the perilous standoff.

A submarine riddled with mesmerizing toil, they peddled the depth gauges,

The taps turned off, the helm a burst bubble.of deciept

They ridiculed the stamina settled, the hydroplanes blew

They set, the boiling hard seas, the lust of the river, the inlet valve leaked,

The lust for a foul tale, a deception of periscope hide the baron mire,

The rivers of bilge, the seas calamity, the rattle of bilges

The pumps they stayed open, the reactor plagued a nuisance,

The core a meltdown resounded the pittle valve

The sub exploded, a fusion of elasticity wreaked a havoc

THE SWASH BUCKLER

A swan of tide the main style flies the sail it furnishes.

The pageantry swelters, the needle a Glim blade shatters the solace.

A worm pencil in the gut, a worm flies the mast.

A scimitar blends, the ketch applies a symphony.

A truss of needle, a cutlass devours the character.

The fervor of sting, the glass eyeball foretells.

The Greek charm, the oars oh men! The oars! They do repeal the Shepard

The steed of foul, the moat of shackles, the oars! Men, oh ah the oars!

The trade winds blew a harvest, the skipper yells ahoy boys.

The valor oh ahoy! He preys the lather the riches of wealth.

The captain of blood, he steers complaint.

The ladies do hallow the victorious, a barbarous scourge swelters.

The rivers of silence, a climber aboard the masts.

A silkworm he plunders, the ships' captain he relinquishes the pattern.

The lady, the Santa Marie, the soapbox 'abhors a compromise.

The Celt old bluebeard he climbs the balustrades.

The heathen pirate scrubs the belly of riches.

The rosy of the keel, she bent the whip, the pull of the haul.
The graveyard bounds with old seamen aboard.
The ship a tonnage of spectral passage north, the East Indies blew.

RASPUTIN

A noble haired Cossack, he romanced the quail, the ladyship she smiled
He jeopardized the pony, softly does it, my dear!
The saddle is a Wentworth of the ladies smiles, the Rasputin he says my lady of clouds
The fondle I requisite I needs of a romantic evening ahead might I touché the frog
I have acquired a taste, a romantic evening of pleurisy, a lady of twilight.
Though does the Czar! He ferments; I dig the contemplativeness of a spider.
A cockroach hounds my bewitcher of sour!
The saints have adored thee, I mirror the fantasy
I realm the noble the rich man's idol! The arisen bequeath of saints he yelled.
He cried the Russian nobles, a pioneer. The Prussian royal family.
A Heathen logo of Mice! The ladies adored his sympathies.
A league of a kinship, the Czar peddled a romance.
He is a fountain of strength, a fundamental of notary republican idol.
The Spanish knew him, a noose they acquired, to stretch his neck.
They ferment his infrequent smiles, the spout to which the colonel cries.

CASANOVA

The castile of conquest', a Casanova of blemish'
He roved the style, the tide of spontaneity he roved.
The shield of the ladies, the duel he fought, he bled the foil.
He scabbards its recluse of prowess I fountana the dread
He flight a dove, he jovial the needle innermost.
The fields of honour I devour the riches of homely peasant
The Princeton of vermouth of sparkling red, he drank to the ladies.
The dowry of women's finery, the bush I say, is mightier than the sword!
The womanish of glamour I bravado the conceited ape!
I claim thy sword its recluse, jeopardy lay mine its wise!
I doest the whole reprimand to the swoop, my ladyship of resentment

THE PASSENGER FERRY

The rip pardoned her coastline, a ferry the Sorrento ferry.
The port Queens Cliff ferry they broke the tide.
The paddlers they motioned the Point Lonsdale.

They boast the giant of Plymouth Rock, the pinnacle reef.
They bass the straight, the heads off pinnacle rock.
The shipwrecks bemused the twin sisters, the pledge of iron
The captain stowed the ferry, a yacht they staved the reef.
The sailors remote, a skipper the giant swells, they revel the draught.
The collision capsized the boat; the ferry rode the wild of squall.
The lighthouse sat, obeyed perilous beginnings.
The seamen moved the base of the lighthouse.
The pilot cried alls aboard, the lifeless!

THE SORRENTO FERRY

A Queenscliff ferry, a barge of passengers they huddle.
The giant squall a heathen of funnel smoke, the boilers refused
A rip torn the engines cried, the flank engines thrust
The flow of the diesels, the stink of engine room bust.
The propellers they flounder, the haunted catacombs they bury.
The midst of grey monsters, the bilge of burden.
The haunted sea, they fathom the menace, the sea swells
The bellowing tides, the ferry shuttles, the weather it catacombs the tide
The longing shadows of a shattered dawn.
The sea a bucket of salt, the dry pan of haunted blessings, driven the wild.
The ketch flowed, the captain he broke the pass.
The passengers weep the awesome array of tide.
A yacht he blossoms, the huge draught of wave, 30 feet trench,

VISTA AVENUE

The night it flows a pardon, fruit of the vine
The wine of Vista, the Monsoon, the Yacht
The flowering petunias they blossom
The wilt of the flowers of spring, autumn abundance
The rosebuds do open the floral nightingale
A bow breaks, the courteous Mrs. Cameron reviles
The roger stakes a claim, a sport the trick to gum,
A dwarf of cotton wool buds, they chatter.
The lantana it creeps, the idol chatter of silkworms.
They fond the sparkle of grub, the chatter of love' birds.
They foreshadow the creeping dew, the waver of hello!
The mansion in the studious pardon, the raucous cry.
Annie, you've forgotten the corn syrup!
An Ian Cameron rose of flora, he stirs, the town of monk.

A Nigel cries the Rancher has an affront, the bushy is here!
The kitchen area follows the dining of catacombs.
The steed of Buckinghamshire ointment rub
The butler idols, the Scotsman deeds, the fashion of old stingy
The black fellow has come to town!
The biker wants old Angela of Philomena-flower!
A girl whips her favorite blouse.
She wanders the gateway of Cameron-reserve.
The odyssey of pathways, the glen of fjord, and the car is rioting.
The boy' of her dreams has come to stay.
A marriage is on the cards! He confronts the Cameron's.
Is she pregnant! A wolf of overseer, he ferments the biker.
A wow! He wants the girl, a paradise of dry footing.
No girl of mine is going out with a leprechaun!

THE ANDES

The survivor of the crash he remembered.
He stowed the baggage, the locker he shed.
The blight of snowman's tuppence, the plane launched a pocket 737.
A plane set for doom, a pencil of pitch.
The airways cluttered the plane it flew.
The reckless of antiphony of slide, a pledge to Penn-brook grove
The primrose stow the passengers felt a bump.
The plane hovered the mount,
The Andes said fly me through the resolute beginning of a flight.
They plagued the snow, the bomb exploded
A passenger fell the window, the aircraft streamed the patch.
They survived a living, the each other, the blinding Ointment
The survivors bleached, the range foundered, they lived

THE GHOST SHIP

The ship worth of sail, the tramp steamer of wild oats.
The sledge of Bacchus ferments.
The Bermuda straits it sailed.
The oars beneath they paddled the Sail, the whip it whirled.
The Bacchus rules the waves, the sloth! The call cried.
They sung a tune of Beatrice, the gang Broderick plank, they threw o'board
The bright eyed floozy she wept, the lady of the bow.
The whip they played the backs of the slave.
The grief it whirled, the snowcaps stooped

The cat of nine tails they bled the grapper-wine dry, the back it rent
The brass ring about their feet, the ankles bled
The poison they drunkard, the keg of sour dough they famished
The bilge ran dry, the hermit they needle the prey.
A Roman he catacomb the brick inlay of thirst
He grosses the Poseidon, will reap your summer's day!
The grapper they drank, the Hearn of salts they politely added
They pillaged, the whaler of that mighty tug
They boast, the languishing pride, the effigy IHVH the standard they flew.
Thy will conquer, thy will kill thy blessed shitfaced, the plague and plunder.
Sailors die, too a cause, I am will save you!

SOCIETY

A pledge to the gods, the mighty Zeus.
The gods will dwell the fiercesome blight.
The terror whipped the seas of Poseidon.
The foundry spelt a choice, the grenadier
The mask of guilt, the guardians replaced those, the temple of the Jew.
He rid that choice of sacrament, Romany of republic.
A encamp of stolen childlike memoirs.
The multicultural of society's river of squirm.
The spirit of the Bacchus a right of condemnation.
The rogue butterfly myth forgotten splendor.
The zeal the common reproach of all evil, the society of languishment.
Zeal of political nonsense, a monstrosity of giant.
The land of gayety, the gender of ruin, the treatise of patriarch.
The motionless tide of free for all!
A gender, the women have not, they spoken loudly!
The political correctness a policy to prevent the idol extremes of youth.
The riches, adulterated the fur, the shoals they speak louder than words.
The theosophy of unadulterated giving, the right to support ones own.
The egotistical vendetta of extremes, the vision of coital marriage.
The heathen they lay dead, of envisioned people's mirth, the vile.
The jeopardy of idol corrective ness, the death for the Brutus.
The Judas will coerce the blameless frog, the scoundrel shall find those.
The death of the peddle of Bacchus, the fruit of jeopardy
Their blameless cock fight, the sellers have paid they boast, the entity

MAXIMILLIAN THE ROMAN

He fought the scabbard, the Roman Empire.
The senate bilged the sail, the arrow defamed the privilege!
The oars they drilled the pike.
Rogue seamen he scourged, the frigate spelled, danger
A dagger plunged, the affidavit snipe, the retched sailor
The depth of an arrow they snow, the tribune of sentencing
He ploughed. the heathen advance, the Jews they fought a war of sour.
The 40-year war the scout of legion the blameless frog of Caesuraerer
The blank of scimitar, he brazed the nickelodeon
The seasons a blind pumpernickel, the bludgeoned scabs
The course of the arrow in flight, the spider witnessed the episode
The Claudius of vicar he cagy a ripe
The tribune fights the guile, he bastard the grief.
The olden empire, the bowel frontier they plagued.
The thirst for blood gouged, the scimitar
The hornet of greed, the lust for gout the grueling slave
Have no-rights, a mutinous scab, and the breadth of liquor
The Caesar he romanced pomp
The edge of a cutlass bore

CLINT

An American actor of acclaim.
He composed a direct of abundance of fame.
He toiled the stage of opera with a horse of no name.
He rasped his first with rawhide, a western of Sergio Leone.
He played the cowboy flicks; he drove the Italian of western follies.
He cowboy the American studios cried.
A memorable José Wales outlaw.
He played a second fiddle to his wife of new.
A Sondra-Locke in the *Dirty Harry* Mexican films.
The Gauntlet and *Two Mules for Sister Sara*
His potshot the bandit his films of *Sudden Impact*.
And *Dead Pool* as the stubborn, tough guy.
The cop they couldn't kill, a wouldn't quit; he waged a war on crime.
A forerunner from his days as a steel worker.
He found a new wife his spaghetti another western hero.
A far from the days of *Rawhide, he* married a quarrel, reaped a single, he retired bullion.
With *Million Dollar Baby*, a list of play, the virgin sands of Iwo Jima,
The page opened, a web site his father would be proud

THE GUNFIGHTER

A José of gunfighter he played
A forerunner of outlaw of public enemy number one
A shattered marriage, he rebuked
A docile of western folk lore they played.
A spaghetti western, the Two *Mules for Sister Sara.*
His motion picture, the farmer of the confederate army.
He stole the silver screen with a blank of notoriety.
He claimed they did it wrong, branded he escaped.
A gorilla he campaigned the notable, a stage and screen debut.
He parched the Glim, the methodology
He crossed the plank of boardwalk with *Sudden Impact.*
He newly married a parched wife of screen and stage.
An impact of double trouble.
He opened a ranch in Arizona, he married again
The Good, the Bad and the Ugly he played.
A temper he orchestrated the actor guild.
He sought, the action hero of the old west
A dirty Harry Callahan, he roughed the flat footed cop.
A gun he toted the hero of *Sudden Impact* and tank of love affair.
The western hero, he close eyed a Herculean feat.
The double action thriller abundance of etch
He scattered a wed of tight lip fantasy with a gauntlet.
He rattled a bread of silver hit on stage.
He cried, the adventurous *Million Dollar Baby,* he won two academy awards

THE RIGHT STUFF

They flew those wielding hornets.
The edge of the rainbow, the flat deck at 2000 feet.
They prose the China crossing, they blazed the rocket chair.
Their last hope the chute blossomed
They flat stick at the hope chest, the Texas pride, the lollypop drove.
They blatant the missile, the corkscrew fired.
They sailed the stroke of fire, the Tomahawk be startled the crew.
The simulator fired a rocket propelled grenade.
The Nancy dry footing, the proverbial, it blew up!
They clamored aboard, the Easy-chair, the sky torn with fear.
An x2 spy craft at stratosphere, it simulated the rocker
They laughed as the basin launched the simulator to the Apollo mission.

They peddled the old rocket, the dummy
They carried the mire, the swamplands of dry pan the chair, the rocket lift
Paradise chairlift, they begged the sickness altimeter.

THE MISSING MAN

They flooded the specter of space, the chapter in the book, from grace
They reviled the benefit, the chariot of drowse
The wise man saw the missing man, he floated in space
The malady of space, the frontier they curbed the space.
The lookout they reaped, they flew about the sun.
A time travel they progressed
The space of shuttle mission 67 they laughed
A said, a paragraph in time, the circular sphere of space.
The $e = mc2$ the lookout spied, the motion of rampant derelict.
The craft orbited the sun; they pancake the planets, the orbital universe
They scorched the earth, the robot of intensity.
They grabbed the time doctor Spock, in 1972. he delved
The Helio of spatial frontiers, the rumor of parable
He claimed the isometric conclusive of irrelevance, the Time-ship
The ship landed in Central Park, New York unlike 2014
The dim reproach, the craft it hells, the motion of time
They masked the ship, a accelerator it rampant the device it built
An organic memory of features, to fly the spectrum
They clawed the time frequency of yellow spectrum
A parable of circular lapses, the b= star chart, the climb it steadied.
They stone the idol, the nuclear warship, the enterprise.
They caught a parable of time, the star-chamber, needs attention.
The sacred onyx stone, the particles of light shuddered
The neutron beam particles of sunlight fusion
The neutron beam of light particles

THE LAWLESS

They pillaged the envelope, the stardom they pickled.
Said old flattery nuisance, dread the old whistler!
He succumbed the rattler, the cosines raiders the Jesse James.
He fast draws the bit in the horse's mouth.
He fired a whistler faster than he drew a jerky, he whipped that damn thing
He proved nothing, he closed the old, and he laughed the shell scrape.
I smoked the 10 outlaws, they docile the clues into the bleeding hole.
I shot the pigs; they drove a pike down, the shot ricochet

The holy Shepard hole, the 45 lariat they laid the simple bitch, into a strawberry
They sunk the teeth the old digger riot, the plum in the hole.
A messy stew of boil the carcass
A green man told the raiders, they smoked a Goldie she welt a Boer.
He sneered the old saloon jack they stayed
The gambler bet a pug nickel with a spade up the sleeve.
He shot first a redeye; he slammed the pea knuckle down the elbow.
I made the meat he curdled the wire, he grabbed the sleeve he died

THE FORGOTTEN GENERATION

The 50's a generation of flawless idols, the favor of doc miller
The pattern of whim, the La Bamba of Ritchie Valence, he cried
The big bopper, the stray of rock and roll music, he played, the baby!
The eloquent sixties, the Seekers, the Oxford party streets.
The Nat King Cole, the Crooners steadied, a recording device
The Pacemakers rolled a clandestine, the dell tones laced
The three pennies, they eloped a wartime of music.
The blend of Buddy Holly, cried Betty sue
The stream of the big bands of dance Glenn Miller big band
The Boston pops of luster, the performance of silken misfortune
The screen antics, the war torn of Dean Martin, the duo of Jerry.
The nightclub singer, the estranged of bop, the garbage tin lids
The garbage can lids, the three pennies
The Jolsen, the crybaby antics of real time, a travesty of peddler.
A shoe shines the snake oil of Bobby Limb
The sad tale of Bing Crosby and Nash the idol.
The Moody Blues laughed the idiosyncrasies.
The three seasons of Natasha Kaminski
The herd of stone, the peace generation, the real-time blues of popular music
The Andrews Sisters called a time out of republican nightclub.
They wrote letters from home, the Korea of stock.
The gross time allowed, the Johnny O'Keefe he sung an aura of melody
The season of died, laid back, the grease of Bobby Darin.
The beach they combed the popular abuse, the beach boys played
The Four Seasons anecdote The Supremes they starlit

THE TREES OF SPRING

Like idols they played, the thunder arose, the darkness frontiers
The seasons of spring the Odessa of plague, trees have eyes
The blackness of ordeal, the jackal he heard

The Odessa of splattered, the motion steady
They plagued the hot summer breezes, the ladies pertinent
The catacomb jungles of awareness plundered.
The waver of lovers permit, the longing of spite
The season of autumn they arose the giant furnaces
The blend of colors, the contours of the faded shadows
The patriots of winter horizons, they publicly denial, those wielding shadows
The rose it satire the glen, the Greek an astonished of glum
The needles of saturated midst.
The blown ordeal, the summer they repose
The petals sadly retorted the nickel shed a tear.
A outspoken the petty of fauna, enveloped a sparkle a shed

THE SPINSTER

Her vale the manservant, a Hotchkiss of gentle
The aroma of Kleenex, she beautified her surroundings.
She fell, a love of kisses sweet the mildness.
The aroma she replicated the tidy of the soldiers.
The diggings she beheld the tidy, her knit, gray craved the spoils.
The tempera of fabric, the wedded bliss she noteworthy, the pleasantries.
The sisters affect of studies, a fallen web of suspense.
She gratified the romance; the plague darkened her Pots-dash expression on life
The frilly negligee, the flowing grays of her curly bronze hair.
The soldier tried a comfort of strain, the paddocks they romanced.
A occasion of ethereal conduct, unbecoming a woman of stature.
She mild the soldiers grace
A gratification of laurels, deeply seated romances.
She felt a passion, a groom the stature of her elegance.
She drove at odds to another, a kindly mother, and the kids.
They laughed the unmarried woman of act.
She encouraged his driven outlandish ways.
A courteous freedom, stayed a polite gesture, she welcomed a kiss.
The boyfriend he died, the wars they took the tide

BELVEDERE

He named the slippers, a Belvedere of conscience.
He drove the pickle barrel, he woe, he knifed an elegant, the Austrian Alps.
He gazed the couch of Satan stir, he downed a stubby of cold ice.
A carpenter by trade he waxed the pride his Alexandria a stone, the pug.
The broody boys he hung out, a pure, he staved cotton underwear

Slender-Pickens winchelsea.fort
I 'm a drunken scumbag, the peddler of moonshine.
Me and the boys we drunkard, the swine of ointment!
We broke the still remote the toil, me Chris' of Truckee acclaim.
He delved deeply the pocket rye, the brewer's ale.
The still' of army eminent the party, old Reds dog the swine.
I'll pardon the French lip gloss, they brew the pink bastard.
The tankard of Raymond's' the wheelchair Burt's place.
His Olsen Place a drunkard, the prejudicial witness.
The pardon the wag, the pleasure, he worked the flavorsome swills
He ate the Kentucky red eye for tea for tea tonight
He woke a stray dog; he curdled the boy's home.
He broke the whiskey bottle over their heads
The mob they cried a hit gun, the contractor bastard his kettles and run.
He drove the Billy of Kentucky red-dog
The old Brian, a cowboy hat, a slick overcoat.
Sympathy to the cause, the red he stabbed with a kitchen knife

THE PIAZZA EMPORIUM

Mr. Abernathy a strange servant of the krauts.
He collaborated the Nazi regime, he stole the meats
The diggers thought primrose he stared, the growth.
On the side of his head, he belched
The olive branches of Open-ware, he staved the picket wire.
The Berlin they cried, they dared he picket the grass.
He strolled, the Austrian Alps, he chased the Germans
He grouses the rummaging bottom of flout.
He caused an immigrant, the shootout they shot the dawn bomb run.
A mosquito bomber they raged, the autumn leaves of Constantinople.
They pardoned the grape, the olive branches withered.
They boast of wine of grapper seed oil.
The oil of nipple, a grape the ranks of the vines.
They peddled the stout, they crushed the grapes
The summer's crop came, a prune neck tie.
The olive of partisan of Nazi killers.
They hid the slopes of the orchards growth.
The summer's crop was not yet finished.
They drove the invasion, the orange picker he came.

JOHN THE BUTCHER

He staved the frontiers of the butcher boy
He asked the emperor of piazza store; the boys' need a poker tonight.
The fellowship, the native toil, and the john he wrote a deed
They chastised the rule, the humdrum, and the boy from across the world
He crowed the Czechoslovakian, the clamor of grotesque.
He Wilfred the nanny of the catholic church, a RC of catholic at birth
He famished the frozen beef cattle, the estranged, and the eggs of climate.
The Italian of Greek community, had a hazy day of it
The church they paraded, the latest of Virgin Mary.

IAN AND SHARON

The VC valiant he rode, a stallion of proof, a Rabbit-proof-fence.
The valiant he tore, the bush he drove, the needle of kosher
The throttle he shed an idol sixpence, the league of generals, the boys'.
He couched her little people, a Sandra he wed a grimace of shallots.
He cried the reel to reel, a stereo he played, the Rock and Roll played.
He laughed the eight tracks stereo, he showed the darling
A time he sped the motor oil, a dime a dozen
He showed the mother an in law, a baby shower he fell.
The father, a Vietnam veteran of the war.
He pardoned the frankness of a boilermaker.
He pardoned the liqueur, a black Russian, a Kailua and coke.
He debased the Joe and his car, he padlocked the bomb.
The garage he smoked, a collision
An orphan he shadowed, he left Sandra at the motor inn.
He sounds the rule for a Sharon of facet, the baby left the shower.
He boast the duel, a Sharon she wept the tide.
The boys they taxidermy a effortless stagger, they plunged the publican a crawl
The laughter thread, a Mount Pleasant road, they Skin-deep.
The Monroe's they fled the dickens for a lost soul.
They fashioned the thread of decency, the Ian plagued the plenty picnic

MARIE & COPPO

The stolen romance they enveloped a tit bit.
The Marie they played a horn of sounds, a mood
The singular Louise she banqueted a levy of surety, an 18 year old she wept.
The singular of raspberry bushes, she maid the boys
The leathernecks she married a Fire-cat she appalled.

The rogue she pulled furniture of beanbags why, yes!
She rode the footing a stream of thanks, a party goers she Clementine.
The Odd-fellow, a youth of preponderance she beckoned a towel.
They skirted the alloy of growth.
The needle they felt they wept for a tidy allowance.
The strong-arm they ruin, the boys they laughed, a Jedadia cooper laughed.
And he sneaked a bundle of Fats Domino.
He wagered the old of 50s genera.
He strolled, the flat, a Billy idol he reveled the tidy little miss.
He stole the pleasant, the archaic remnants.
The smile that launched a fleet of ships, a Helena of troy once said
A mountain man's dream, the scorch-earth, the ships that Sail-title, the loathsome Greeks

THE LAVISH RESTAURANT

A girl broken hearted, the lavish of crime
A restaurant she had patronages.
She climbed aboard the taxi awaiting.
A cry from a boy, she waited a man of the internet.
He cried an Email from Joseph, the plea of the wild.
The rose of duck, a book of Mrs. Dorothy Pinch shot.
She read the well anointed prayer, she told over the web.
An estranged excitement, the Dorothy found a man.
She owned a bookshop, the adversary owned the opposition.
The foxes books superstore of quarry, livened her license to kill
She welled with tears, the man of disapproval, he appeared.
The yielding ape of gorgeous she thought.
The wedlock she became alleviated, the strife in her eyes.
The ape he laughed I called you!
The doctrine she held, the *Forsythe Saga* welled, her anxious breath.
And she approached
He said I stool a malady for your young lover!
Is this rose, the Dorothy Pinch shot, the wedded, of bliss for his!
Just as she promised, they kissed

DENNIS AND JOY

A glimmer of passion they met.
The horseless carriage of discreet and the marital bliss they pledge
The allegiance the lead guitar he purveyed the strange.
The purpose of engagement, their parents a harsh elope.

The caravan they sneaked, the party

They prestige the Karalee Street party of Ian old-bush.

The boast of Yoruba Parade, the wedded they exclaimed.

The tidy now and then, the parent they dismissed the passion

The girl, joy she promised his allowance

She, a fair 16 years old, a blemish on a passion, the rosy cheeks.

They played a disturbance on in-laws they built, a rambler matador

They accrue a whip the old car into shape.

The bridled the incarnate looks, the passions, the stares

They made love the back of the matador.

The cold they caught, a whimper of Wood-fire.

An ecstasy they caught, the back of Ian's panel van.

He drove them the back way, the Ute they beckoned.

They said, I leave a harsh robin, I scout the prolonged ecstasy

The grape doesn't matter; she'll weep the fridge magnet.

The courage built on fear, the parents they besiege the antelope.

They won't care; they married the peek of indulgence

HAROLD AND JOAN

A born tyrant of the lad, a bully boy of the grade.

He ruled Iron-fisted, the wife Joan.

She tried a Ruby she Harriet the Glenn of Fernside avenue

The boy of clover, the girlfriend she laughed.

The boys she raised, the grace from pilfering grove.

She cried the Poppy-fruit, the dismal of pumpkin, she wept

She closed a net of friends, her wagon of deception.

A Montmorency-town-club, the cherished bitter fruit

A grouse of pittance, she smoked the passive angel of dread.

She witnessed the crow fights; she expunged the impunity of apple

The rice of gladly spirited risen, she gladly timed

The wedded of cock crew the fights, the armor of salvation.

Her grandmother, her mother, her Florsheim' shoes, a business partner.

She cried a leper of the Burt Manufacturing.

The empire grew, she handed a check of $30 G's.

She accrues a settlement, the Jon, Don and Denny.

The pocket of the banks, she accorded the faith of Oscar the beetle.

He ran him a silo of grief.

THE BUNER'S

They laughed the Portarlington house, they driven the horseman's folly
The number73 they stool the Harriet, they pilfered the old Harold.
The jack cross, the Winfred red, they smoked the horseman's' cart.
The Cross-Waite, old jack they divulged Joan a dizzy shopper.
She cried Harold; don't follow the league of patron saints'.
They sullied the following, they savored the warm welcome!
They soldiered a will, the swum the cabin into oblivion
The Blue-line-shipping-title, the van they famished, a dry martini
They disposed the will they signed, the fraud they accomplished.
Mum and the kids don't matter! The streak of butterfly gulch.
The passage west, the stream took the initiative, kitchen.
The courts told of a dreary story, Harold Run-a-muck.
He rampant a church he sullied the reverend
The Burt Manufacturing Empire he rode.
A stolen For Pete's sakes, they did not mean it!
They strolled the waters, the caravan they sold.
The old house on the hill, the hound for the dogs.
The Harold jeopardized the hidden loot.
The Ruby he grimed, the etiquette he sublimed
He laughed poor old Joan into oblivion
A memorable pittance, the Holden he sold fleeting memories.

DAN AND JENNY

They played a game, Jenny-scot-free.
The languish the arms, a feral he committed, cried
The Peter he cried a memorable, Scottish working mans grade
They grew the tired old ocean of tears.
The mamma's they desolate the stroke, the calming influence.
She grew a tired old heiress image
Her motherly infatuation in the small child.
She drew a woman closer; the boys played the scarecrow
They loved the old grandmother, the lady of suspense, a rosy glen.
The mother, the lover of the two, the couple found a elderly mother
The jenny wrote a page in her book, the lady of melody
She cried a wedlock of Greek ceremonies, she motherly the love.
The Jenny joined the police, she chased the criminal.
She drove a candy, a Worm'ld security.
The memories of old mamma, she graciously cache remembering
She peddled grief, a widow of a cause, the dear old grandmother.

She tucked a head under tight lip; the elbow sought a lovely old mother.
She sought the reflection in her own mother.
She found a boy; he became a man, a reflection of her very own
Young James, a youth to Butter-field melody, a prosperous of kindness
A reminisce to remember, a police sergeant; she married a fine man
A James the champion at chess, he surrounded the kindness.
He cried a tissue into the footstep, the mother
The boys they played a trick, the canon bare ointment
James he played a police lieutenant, the boys, they ran for cover.
The Dan a detective sergeant, he broke a clock into elite of police
He struggled with the old boy, he met the wheelchair athlete.
He succumbed to the graduate, he laughed the tall man.
He luxury the old girl, he played a game, she caught him out!

SUE AND MARK

A rummaging of fate they glued a fascination for each other.
They bloom hardiness, the fortuitous glimmer.
They shared the limo scène of gratitude, the feverish smiles.
The idol contentment, the measure of a baby
The son they had a baby Ryan of flatulence member.
The family described it, a Sue incapable of suing.
The fate Sue belonged; the society condemned a small child.
A grief stricken, the partisan, the slender, Mark lavished a computer.
He cried how it loved him! He remarked how it should not!
He barked at Sue, the astound, of perishing empathy.
The Wiley he, of grotesque smiles, the Sardinia of contempt.
The docile Sue, she wept, the scholar of pragmatism.
She shoal the boy, she betwixt the omen, the computer loved the Mark.
An empire the rude, he shoal the boy, he stole the fate.
The Ryan ousted the mother, a bleak the benign influence.
The father he wept, and the boy he rode he flew a plane.
The jungles of Africa, he shod the steely grace of contempt.
Zeal he found, a father stricken with desolate beginnings.
He stole the love of reputable hope, engendering spite
He shined the Datson 120Y; he cried the boy should be a nice guy!

THE NAZI HUNTER

A faith of fatherly love, the negligence of pistols club.
The shooter of the Nazis during the war, the bitter feud
He ramrods the stolen relatives, he cried the pack of the KGB,

The intelligence organization, the OHS he cried underground
He ran Old Val Kaminski he doest the pride, he eliminated the russias
The elite the armies, the French stole the etiquette, the fried kipper
He left his family of Prague, he leapt a bard.
They stole his mother; he laughed the war on fascist regime.
With Germany the OHS of underground,
The movement of America of famished he prejudice
The wager he pride himself, the hurt of suffering.
He cried his aunts, the Margeret he married.
He spied the movement; Eliminate the witness
The popular of pride, he immortalized the motif force.
He cried to his mother a lover of whos nowhere
He knew sixty languages, he preyed the scholar, inkling of terror
He met Harold, the best of friends they played the house of portarlington
The beachfront understudy, they wooed a tear for the Germans.
They killed defeatist none, they predator the whole wrechmacht
The understudy of Margeret, she fled with Val, a small child they bet the bushel
She wrote a diary of Tuttle, the boy' she had, the Margeret she levied the cousin.
My boy', a soldier of elite, the strongman of the OHS.
He mammoth oh kill the filthy swine, the Gerry he shot dead

VAL AND MARGERET

He Rasputin the rascal of the war, his hemlock the docile lady.
The Nazis they cried, a fernery of spy Network.
They raged the OHS of under the ground, the spy net
The grave secret he held to the grave
They preyed on the wolf pack, the emblem of scatter.
The hierarchy of the high command, the rage of civilians, he killed Jerry
He stroked the caterpillar, a jump from an Aircraft.
He made a Will, he stowed aboard a freighter bound for the coast
He ramrods the civilian frontiers, he cried the mother
He knew a cache of 30 languages; he chased the KGB into a corner.
He wept the authorities, his gangland the syndicate of the sportsman's almanac
He grosses Berlin, his privy as a spy he loved the lady
He knew the counterfeit general, the rabbit of sage, he eliminated the spy
He grimaced, a sortie of flight over Dresden, he bombed the particle
He flew the Boeing of hornet, the spy he chased, he killed the Prussian
The Jerry Klink he tortured, the meadows of homeland Prague.
He wept the swastika he erased. The lifetime of swastika
The Nazis foothold on Czechoslovakia, he raved the odds.
He married a girl, a Margeret he abode.
The Slavic revolution he ran, too ground he fled to Australia.

LEONIE AND DWAYNE

A tightly knitted web of deception, a river of Caruthers and Dwayne.
A valor of Dwayne goes to work, a 12 hour shift
A Beatrice of lovers permit, the carer of the grade
A degree of flatulence, her bird on the wire
A Leonie unmarried woman of the grade, a woman of Greek sufferance
A pony she loved, the petite Zoë, a malady of trite misgivings
The web of ultra light, the glamour of effectual, grimmace
The satisfeld an excitement gathers, the bitter sweet melody.
A sue of pomp and ceremony, she gathered her blessings.
Glad tidings of frequent, she welds the couple of grace.
A baby' Zoë cries, the night of uproar, the glamour of knitting a shred of pact.
The Ashley borrows the car keys, a trite alley of fiend cries out.
The Subaru blew a hub cap, the engine does the head gasket;
He stays the ex of Glynn, he strove a younger brother,
A Thierry of partisan surrender, in a word, the Tolstoy in Greek,
The mothering of bittersweet, thierry delivers a sermon,
The wife she must can do, a director of the clan
A bishop of the Pentecostal church, a fleabag of tongues swept the sanction wild

LEO AND DORIS

A Phelan of wedded bliss, the church is on!
The study of thalamic resources, the needle at pains
The trident of the spear! The Dutch of Leo, his clavicle.
The days of old, the first AIF, the war he painted a clerk.
The wedded of attorney he slouch, the chaperone he melted, the girls
Vera Elaine and Phyllis they rode the donkey down the sheep's back.
The Sleep-out they tired a glimmer, a François they begged to differ.
They bought a Bank-house, a 615 Bell street they bellied ingenuity.
The old timers they peddled, a penny farthing
They show pony a velvet cure, the tried of test
The pound note for a silver dumpling of Coal gas.
They rebuked a passage of timelessness, the tide of laurels
The plague of Doctor Smith, the Johnson is next door.
The tripe pudding of pot with zeal of choric acid.
The timer set, the fuel a wet handkerchief, the dory she grasped.
The wedlock the REX HOTEL they built a haven.
The daughter Joan, the buttress of Holden they forlorn the powder of faces.
The POP went to work the old clavicle, Freddy disk the shine.
He stormed blasted Freddie, he mother the Shepard

GEOFF AND BARBERA

Geoff a mad Essendon supporter, he reviled in the game of VFL.

He toad the mixture of footy, the goals they umpired the spirits lifted.

Barbara she left a profound interest, she stole her chaperone,

She stayed an elderly mother, the father died, they reproached gentry.

The founder of the Geelong football club.

They shook the pea in the bottle they bled.

The Miramax of cinema fed a vigil, the usher and the beetle they loved.

The drive, the wintry lights of Dandenong.the mountain top lovers

The girl she whimpered the lights of Dandenong.

The heights of the sunflower restaurant they dozed.

The Center-city-flats, the nightfall fell, she fell in love

The city heights, the motel of flats they shared, a opinionated grief

They come a cropper the Limousine, faltered a bedpan

They loved as teenagers at the cinema, the screen antics

He laughed a foxy lady, the deem to have met, the party

The Aussie accent soured, the ledge of indecent, the naked fruit.

They cherished the blanket scene, the revelry.

The sin of love is a truce of fine living.

The Barry restaurant, the Elizabeth Park of dirty dealings

The woman you love, a skirt for the fiddle, I prefer a girl

The skin deep of flowers, a hazy of furniture they eloped.

Treason of Winston, Burbank's Junior.

MARGO AND MARK

They met De Witt designs, the plague of Caruthers and Vine

He caught her golden, bronze tipped hair.

She drew a breath, she cried her parental consent.

She said my father works the clavicle of design, the De Wit signs.

The gifted mimic, he closets her blonde tips, the butte of negligee.

The necklace tidied her lips tender and sweet.

Her guilt of fed her minx, a stamina driven ecstasy, a courtesy from grace.

A fervor she spoke, a natural saturated sound,

A gentle mildness awakened her starlit globe.

The eyes they patterned, the cry of the wild

Temperance she mattered not her silken negligee.

Her darkened pocket, her silken of brooch

They met, the Rattler of Red, the train, the boy her brother

A court of wedded she wondered, a prince charming she awakened.

She tidied the mascara; she dressed a slim line courtesy of act.

She broke an eye shadow covering the furnace, the wallow

THE VISION OF DAWN

She erupted a silence, the Claude of Constantinople.
The acclaim of Pam, the wife and three daughters.
The webbed feet, flat feet of New Guinea, he fought the Japanese.
The 113th battalion, the Papua New Guinea, the bomb exploded.
He leapt a phosphor bomb they sent him Home.
He beached the whaler, the June he lavished a crime
The carol she married Michael McKee.
The band they played, day and night, the space invaders
The bands, the bred sympathy, the bass jeered harmonic.
The band they played, a season of four they played.
The dawn a bright eyed florescent teenager.
They remembered the mechanic the lowly car.
The city lights they cried, the diggers attest
They delivered the loaf, the milky shed, the horse and cart.
The Greenhill's road, the Diamond creek amassed a Levine shire
The four seasons of malady. the check he wrote to dawn, the patriot of collie.
They engaged a party, the thought he was, the juke of merriment.
They juggled a married, they cried the orchestra

THE PRIVATE AND THE LEFTENANT

A lieutenant of be be quieting of odds.
A method of tried and tested, an officer youth training college.
She laughed the boy, she broke into tears.
Her eyes amassed guilt, met his forlorn sadness.
The treacle ran a fluent, the soldier a private of the army.
He smiled the regulations, the Queen he beckoned.
A footloose, he sadly remarked, the boast of my tender haven.
The rouge she commented, the eyes plummeted,
The guise of fervor the cheesy grins.
The famished of frozen stares, a longing of street trees, wavering in the wind
She buttered his bread, she cried a gorgon of sympathetic.
The officers stared astray, the league of generals.
They broke, a heartless remark, the saturated remark
The girl she cried a pink affidavit, a grim reminder.
A solace to stare, she resolute his
A battle of wits, the end of snout, a repugnant nettle of wings.
She sadly purported, I have a moment, and your tealeaf is mine
She sadly wept, the cry, a tear, a glen shattered the moment of despairing

A well-oriented snuffle, the badge of rank, a Queen's regulation.

She backhanded a swoop, a needle of pair.

She ripened the stare became a grimace of infatuation, they loved' the oceans of ferment

A NIGHT TO REMEMBER

A Dianne of spontaneity, she reveled in the sin

She glowed, a city of lights, the parking they borne.

She growled a harshness of belittle, a personality crazed the love and affliction.

Her toast pride of a person, she cried the strongman of the Transport corps.

A women's royal Australian army corps she wrangled the finesse.

A dispute held her in contempt; she riled the ocean, the brother frank.

She drove a Torana; a sporty jargon accelerated her cheat.

The war of attrition she defamed a spirit, a seasoned web she wept.

A Disco she went, the bronzed Australian defamed her orchard.

They kissed a memorable of glamour, the excitement gathered.

The boat too slow for her resonance,

A little cousin grew her tyrant, the lady of the night

She established the Westgate, the defining moment, the Mitchell drive.

She cried the house, a said, tiny flat she numbered her young.

A snail of corrupt biddings, the corporal she called Frank!

Civically minded as discreet, she perched the boy's laceration.

Pursuant to her grove, the fernery lavished the punishment.

The guise she stared her golden daisy wheel of infatuation.

A chain, a woeful is be startled her grief; she found a fond starlit grove

The Wellington he grimaces welled, the pumpkin pie to Grandmothers'.

FILOMENA AND A MOMENT TO REMEMBER

She gauged her womanish feelings of gratitude.

She fought the edge of the rainbow, her tears stayed there with him.

She cried the High-five on the TV, the escalator ride developed

She repertoire a dear friend, she cried, Hello mate! A raucous cry.

She groaned the sexual connotations, a sigh of reckoning.

She loved his spy; he glazed the eyes for her warmth.

Her Gravy-train she beheld, the pathways to her infirmity

She cleaned the cans, the Victoria bitter, the pub he belched

Tonight! Her velvet a promiscuity of cry baby.

She came to him, the middle of the night.

A romance differing, the boy needs a pot of grass.

She felt things should be kept in place, her petty lounge

She beat a Red robin to the draw, her ballet toil of her toys

Lard, a boy she cried, the dear old mate, he waits up for me!

She went the Heidelberg inn, the prince she admired.

He went away; she cried his lap, the derogatory palace of dreams

She drove the Toyota; he fondled his while I chased mine!

She waited a robin red breasted moment, the wasted nights

She depraved a moment, they stripped naked, and she fought every moment

The desires, the showmanship, the shower they remarked.

She cried the breast I have is not meant for yours.

She tied an angry look, uncertain of his moment of desire

JAN AND MARTY

A Jan of three, three girls and a boy, they denied an essence of tragic.

The owl hoots a car accident, the Kyabram lad flew

The in laws favored his way about town.

A Kyabram lad with long hair, he bellowed the boys to dinner.

He moonshine the lager, he rebelled, the Working-mans-club

He belt the belly of pork, he suffered the alienation of trifle.

The wife he valor, he suffered a meat and potato fan

His growth a beard and a long hair do

He string fellow Hawke a docile, the wife rummaged the stove.

She cooked a beastie, a antelope of fair given's

She driven wild, a passion for the pool, a lake of tears

She romanced the ocean of tears, a lapsed memory of quatrain

She passionate the rival, the Bill Street boys of Kyabram

She established a rule, sympathetic to the herd.

A farmer he laid the griddle-iron, glorified beef cattle

He fathered a strong element of lovely boys

She staved the portion, top cricket players, a Melbourne supporter she raised.

THE WITCH

A fiancé of Albert, she cried a wheelchair, she favored none

She languished the pain of others she drew short straw.

Her velvet strong the entourage of bottle shops

A cousins Louise to her Frank the brother of Hells angels.

She choked the routine of allowances

She found a pocket-penny, she logy the pet snake.

She driven a whaler through paradise curve

She found a cobbler at arms, the Freemasons logy her perusal of men

A toll laughed the witch of bay leaves

She drove a pickle jar routine to Paris, the cobble stone roads of Amadeus

A wept of drive her mini to Paris, a drive to motor her desires of Kansas
The brothers Grimm they stowed her in the tuft of shy.
She burnt Bay leaves, the banishments of book thereof
She stole a hobbyhorse, she rendered the dark fiddle
The golden calf of upheaval, the hound of Baskervilles

THE GIRL ON THE BUS

He drove the wildcat, he hovered the sleepless.
The long drive to Sydney he slept the trucking stop
He caught a roadhouse smile, the fox's lair, a grub steak
He cache a small girl, he cried a fast drive
He crashed the car, a wall of ice, the dreadful paradox of sleep.
The car fell apart, the expressway it gathered speed
He crowded the Gosford expressway, a wreckage he ape
The cliffs they tore the car, a haven of signal to sleep,
The rocks jutted the steep climb, the wreckage it flew a jumo crash
He caught a bus, a Sydney sider laughed.i have you intoxicated
A girl shy, she made his day a tiny bit smaller.
He wept her smiles, drove her into submission.
She pondered a wait, she cried the grease haven.
A scallywag, she broke into tears, he wandered alone,
The girl from Paramatta road lost, he wept

CHRISTINE OF RAILWAY

She drove him wild, a stare of conglomerate, misgivings
A rip in her skirt she flaunted her bikini, she cried let me rest
A maiden of love, she wept his knee, she paddled his leg
She cried her brother; he broke into tears, the terror Australia
The bastard from Broadmeadows, the Zachary of warmth.
Her pocket met his, a sensual decree, her pride the notion
The wheelchair she sat, a pledge of midst rang her bell
She cried the trial; the police watched intent on a Robbery-under-arms.
She pocket his wallet, she cuddled a cuticle, she stole the bootie
She mammoth a breast, the mammary she soaked his cloth.
They hardened the halfpenny midstream the skirt.
They kissed till a dark figurine of Chopper Read stooped
She broke into tears, her wet embrace she gladly profound.
The guilt edge of finery, she promised a Saturday night.out

A TRAIN FULL OF GIRLS

A bright-eyed loner, a scatter of Adidas runners, a trainload of girls
A scorecard of work, the footy of TAB, a greasy coveralls
He reveled the tidy footing, the scope of two black sheep.
He cries as he boards the lorry, the Red-rattler,
A Victoria rail of trail blazing, he reaps the tow, the sneak a sleep she blazed
He begs the downer, asleep the train, he awakens the girl,
Not one but zillions of women, they dispose the misnomer as a junkie
A heat of exchange, a harsh word of abuse, but Eddie you will do!
A woman cranks the tired old Juliet, a scene erupts a girl laughed
They all join in! The verse of St Peters he cries
The girls they pocket the change, the soldier of strap the boots all greasy.
They will not want me! A girl cries why not!
A greasy boiler suit, the stout of VB can of bitter.
He transforms the bootie for a golden carriage of dreams
She smiles then leaves the heated display of lovers permit

THE GIRLS OF 7TH TRANSPORT SQUADRON

They foundered the wares, the Ors mess they occasion a wedlock
They played a game of Pumpkin-pie, the wedded mess
They longed the boy, a man of the Mess, the Phil he exchanged words
The pumpkin she bellowed, the boys have a say, and can't we swap a meet!
They cried till dawn, the spectator she rampant
The gorgeous Karen from Tillamook, the Dianne of stud
She wept, the Corporal of the Mess, he dozed, the boys;
He swapped the nurse for a sex change, they wept the ardendorf,
The sergeant of arms, the stray dog of Wild-card, he kissed them all
He stroked the catch 22 he peddled profanity; Wise old duck!
He wise the old chook, the marine he peddled a suffice of Ben-gay
The girls they huddled around the sturdy lieutenant Rouse
The chook enveloped a married, a chook lampoon the crazy eyed Australian
And Sharon she woke them all up, he cried the virgins mattered not!

THE BRIDE GIRLS

They clover the leaf, the bride she blushed,
She wandered the log fire restaurant, the woodfire they cried.
The Paris fashion statement they observed.
They met a frog, a wheelchair, till they wept,
The kissing bride, they held together Janine she befuddled, a chat they had.

The obscure they weld her senses she climbed, a cot
The wheelchair athlete she cried, a bemuse of terror crossed her eyes
She sense the herd, the boys they warned the mac bride sisters
The flashing Deidre, the opposing twin sister, they instill meadows,
An outlook they broke a sparkle in the eye, one to the other
The last boyfriend they giggled, till the sparkle of hearsay.
They wept, the taxi, of wheelchair, a bus deferred, the girls shared a remark
Their pleasantry, the visit of rule, they kissed a wet heart.
The cross of ladies they murmured they cried we will and we wont
The taxi levied a parental consent, we love the guy

THE GOSFORD TICKET GIRL

He climbed aboard the sneakers they wept.
The ticket girl laughed, a rotten egg she board the pass she cried.
A ticket for the sales of lesser morsel, a purple headed nit
A sheep shearer of lesser importance; Approached, the ticket box
A well to do sitter laughed, your a stout boiler maker needs a dirty girl
He laughed I do not suppose you are taken!
My fine girl of my dreams!
She disposed a river of dreams, not for yours!
A cow of horseman's dearest grub for the forsaken of spilt the witchery grub
My boyfriend will blacken the eye of that suppose!
He laughed a spoil; he grew a Lamborghini of mistrust.
He blended the sleek improviser of his dreams
He drove the wet whistle of contempt, he whistled the girl, she marveled the gear.
The black boiler suit, the greasy winds that stalked her brief
She asked is that a bottom dollar you keep;
On the other hand, is that lump in your pants for me!
It is but it isn't your dreams for tonight! He laughed
The soaked panties, the lovers leap we kiss in the cradle tonight
She disposed of nectarine, she cried I lovers leap to your dismay
May I meet you in a dream sequence tonight, the pork is a barrel
Of lovers leap, my fantasy is not for the likes of you she cried

LOVERS ON THE BEACH

Sharon, she glamour the boys, she kept a diary of firm nipples.
She wept a bright eyed, bled a courtesy, she felt a hand
She clamored the rush as the rally driver, she begged.
And sought a love, she cried the man of her dreams
She spied the little man, a title of green eyes

A sister stopped her loving, a discreet Annie she probed deeply
She wept the four seasons, a ballet of progressive stints
They drove the Port Arlington myth of cherries, may I suppose us!
The delight as lovers touched hands, the bunk it boarded, they drove
The ravine of two, the lovers' fortunate, the beach sands, glossy white
The distance unraveled, the eyes focused, each other, the swans leapt
The sad looks, the crying of remake, the bridge of turtle hairline
The boots, the girl she wakened the dream,
She clasped her hands the bunk, he slept above
A longing for lovers' sweet caress, the starlit vigil,
The sparkling web of deception, a momentary lapse of feeling,
The wedlock sparkled, their eyes met, an infatuation

THE QUEEN AND MOUNTBATTEN

She bridled the King, the Edward, her semi the bridle of Blavostock
The agreement they shared a marriage of convenience
The Harry of idol constraints, mercy fed thy mule of esperance
The Duke of Wellington, the queen she bemused
The pride of the Royals the Brittany furs
She barbequed the Ellington of mercy fed
She buttress York Princess Anne a feud
Her cousin Nancy she fed the isle a Wentworth at arms
A horse bridle of bit, a Nancy of clemency.
The love affair, the Mountbatten o' traditional
The boast of the coronation, the partisan of sweet mercies.
The dash for the pool of tranquility demur
The divine the Royal-coach, a sympathetic drove
The ladyship quarrel, a Emmet of silk, the guards remember thee
The grenadier guards the Buckingham palace of many fine mercies
A privy his Excellency ballet, the palladium performance
The scarlet robe adorned thee
The dome of the roof of Windsor castle I remember!
The Remington druid, the colloquial of Rembrandt the walls of bustle.

THE CAFÉ LAWRENCE

The boys they strung a web, until dawn they drove
I am on the way from Sydney they laughed
The credit card limit broken, a sturdy old fellow laughed.
He crowed, the bastion old, the days a bit on the pokey
He laughed the One-armed-bandit, sloshed a schooner

The boat of Cadillac he whispered an ear, kindness gratified.
A greetings, the café girl she laughed, I 'm Dawn of Peters-farm.
The colony of Griffith, English spoken, the dread of picnic grove, they sped
The girl she laughed, do you have a bed for the night!
My downer of tub well spoken English she spoke.
The Dyer of Pick a Box came here!
She wept the loss of a friend

KEVIN AND MARY-ANNE

She abode a pleasant personality
She river the extremes, the pot she smoked a dope
She cried a wino of fruity alexia, she driven wild.
The passion, the motif of the glean she rode a wild pony
To Kevin, the Wangaratta boy, the GV hotel she loaned
Bullion of grant, a Gary of stern, he prods the nuisance
He bilge the TAB, he threw her out
The stallion wild, the bewildered he cried
And he stayed the night drunkard the port of swill
He boast the Lance, a lady, she welled with tears
He blamed the wheelchair bandit
He sure thing the old whip, the girl he cried, he stowed the laughter

BEV AND PAT

A burden they share, a quiet time of the TV
The broken hearts they pledge, he raspberry bushes they despair
A work in the garden, the garden of pat,
He climbs the bushes, the rode a barnacle, he plagues the wife she begs
A cherry she prunes, the meet of the writers group
The Royal-command-performance, the Craig he stripes the short story,
Allan Mathews he plies his trade, the book he so loved,
The Gail of so white the snipe, the picturesque view of the lodge
Of poly François she beckons, a playwright, the motion for Mr. News
He stows a short story, Roger of Murphy he distinguishes himself
The Barbara of cotton fields, the strawberry plucked.
The herbs of the bath of poets; The ladyship entourage
The home for the gayety of verse, complaints to the burrows

MARTINI

Her wedlock the feud, a grape for the kind sir!

She pardons the theorem of who played the orchestration!

She punches the girl, talk to the guy, in the frolic she pardons his frolic

She reaps the bandit, the awfully nice guy!

The wheelchair he grapes, the lodge of piffle eats his supper

The creed of supple he weds the girl, his eyes a fountain of disdain,

He cries tonight my lady of freedom, the mighty have fallen,

The grapes of thy eyes have told a story

She laughs the bosoms, the neck tie, the fairy of the knight the distinguished.

The harmonium of glory she begs to be left alone,

He whispers, the pet glances, and the ride of the life.

To a girl, with as many fruits to her score!

She broke down and cried, he came a cropper

She glanced the beaten egg of fashion straddled

Her perfume of betwixt the passionate looks

A parade of fashion, the Murphy Street of the boys,

He clavesco of the milder set, the drugs, the jazz festival of lights

He expunged her grateful looks, she delivered a sermon!

Look after this person! She asked who beat him up!

THE DATING AGENCY

He paddled the dread, a firm nipple he cried

The crescent flag, he broken hearted wandered

The Flinders Street alleyway, he needle a kindly girl

He flatulent a lady of the mall

His bravado a scenic a Pigeon-hole they cried

Put you in with the ladies they smiled

They melted a one eyed Jack of crosses

The girl he had been, and he pardoned the plight

The blight he suffered a antic, a girl to be married, he joke

A petty ransom a Christian a fed up crying!

She muttered a word of Felix, a gender of passion

She thrived the boyhood charm, the elixir cross she muttered

A married in 30 days she laughed, a cry of croak he laughed

The Wentworth budgerigar they leapt a virgin of collide

The father will not let me!

A SWALLOW AND TIARA

A Brendan and Tiara, a mixed couple
They shed a tear, the boathouse they brills the tenderness
They stole the chapel, a wake they shattered a pearl of constituent.
And fence wire, the Brendan a mad bike fanatic
He chased the girl; he drove the fiber of gloat
He pencils the crime of Home of blameless of geriatrics.
The motif of the house, a pen in hand, a silken potato,
Peeler! a crazy, really a rubber duck
She wrote the western of trio, a boy of esteem, he pillaged her potato crop.
She laughed the bright haired angel.
She despaired the ocean of Fairbanks Junior.
He crowed the larrikin, the Cops chased the bike
He stole the virginity he allowed the western scriptwriter
He drove the cropper into a tale of deception, she followed

SHOWBOAT OF ILLUSION

A lance of gender, a freedom of fanciful wisdom
He plagued a date, the ocean he fed, the Star-struck Wendy at odds
She wept a green of real; she stride a saddler of horses
She found him, the papers corner edge
The companion of dating the service, the whereabouts
Unfrequented fools! The wept of cantankerous moods
The deliverer of spite, a cold beer, a lemon bitter,
Of pride unfrequented by her pride, the woman he loved
My woman of anger, a treasonous of perpetuity of anger!
She sold the slaver of Greek, they built a lemon
A house until dusk, and a brandy soaked in pepper
A cold liquor broke the wine, thrust the hold, she starved the bread
She insisted no more liquor, a broke bed linen
A swashbuckler by trade, a foundry found her pittance
A struggle! She deliberated a rhythm
A wellness of black of tread, the wheel marks, the old Holden
A Brock motorist he foreshadowed

WAYNE AND LESLIE

She broke into tears, a 15 year old she pardoned grace
She felt the love of man she so loved!
A pudding of waistline, she shared an elope of Pigeon-broth

She stew a rabbit a fur of rabid

She clientele the secretary, the typist of 1000 words per minute

She drove the kitten a fur ball she coward the riverboat

A skipper, Wayne, the sledge of magnetism

He whipped the dog, fed it gravy and corn cutlets

She docile the rabbit aware, the likelihood of rarebit and salad,

The dreams of consequence of motherhood, awareness for tea tonight

She died crying awareness, she cloaked a stab routine

She dreamt the river of dreams; they bed the cockles of idol chatter

And the cancer struck her down; Wayne cried

STEVE AND CAROLYN

They met a Disco, a Hangout-bar, and college of the Arts

The frivolous Doctor he method, the stein of beer

He fell; the girl asked a penny for a discreet wonder!

He docile the old penny, she gazed the beautiful eyes

The Carolyn bet you I can sink a dumpling!

The Steve he smithies a foundry of days

He asked the wild, may I have her!

He broke the tears, he stole the pumpernickel

He dozed dray a horse's back, he cried, Can I have her,

She moaned a kidney slice, a boy he sunk the nickel,

She stabbed the heartstrings, he bet you a crime for a night on your own!

She drove the bike away, the slather marshal-nickel, she pony a acquired taste

She took Steve to bed, the shattered romance ended

THE PROMISCUOUS SANDRA

She loathed a steak of cold pepper, she cried an Ian

He crowed the VC valiant, and he drove them wild

The San Ramos, a Pub with no beer

The grub he felt the murmur, he cried they swaggered tale

The daisy, the rally driver he laughed, they chased the old leather jacket

A plea they remorse none, but her bootstraps

They broke into tears as Mick, scouted a brown dog

The headlong into mischief, the pub with no beer, the caravan

Afterwards! They stole the mirrors, the grape they drunkards

The pasty faced, they thumbed a lift

The dogs fault, the excuse the coppers they dread

The man at the pub, he brown dog us out, the car

Caught a rim and a blank horse down

The rubber laughed, they sailed the USS buttress, the oceans eleven
They carried the swollen ranks, the party of friends
They had a hell of a time, they swung a dead cat
The Sandra lay half naked, she treasured his looks
She bellowed, the caught the rally driver unawares, she laughed
You need it! I need it as well! She laughed as Ian threw him out

IAN AND SANDRA

They driven the carriage, the valiant of Ian
The AP5 they signed their names
They played the Bohemian-rhapsody
A Queen, Rock and Roll band they shred the belief, a trip to swill
The drunkard of trio, they laughed, Ian and Sandra
The boys sung a swoon; a Wayne and Joy felt sure
The boys, the mentor Ian they alleged, they ran a muck of dregs and ice cream
They swung a dead cat, they took the rifles, and Ian cried an Owl hoot
The muck ganger does not have a shooters license, he remarked!
A fusilier he grotesque, a bandit from the Royal of pardon the reserves
He laughed how they blew a hole in the wall
He snaked the roads to Sydney, they chased the girl
The Bowie they sung, the *Wayne's World* of song and dance!
A peddle the AP5 car a little harder, they exchanged ideas
They stooped the wayside, the girls they politely added, find a girl!
Mister showman, they snaked a river gorge with no feud
They shotgun a rabbit, the stolen the girl she met with shy old cried
They romanced the girls, the beach party; they slept the back of the car

GEOFF AND SANDRA

He craved the notion for hungering of passion
A fetish he had her pride, the milk of breast
He roasted the fed she bemused her kittens
The Cassie he knew her well, he grouse the cat amongst the pigeons
The young lady amongst the men, she crashed the mirror of fools
The wasteland, he labored the love, the tie of deception
A mate he called her, he marveled her courtesy
He cried the women, he moaned her little person
And he drove her wild, the brother he remarked!
A Passover a fiesta he cried, the beer he drank
The Geoff he played the cricket the boys, on every other day
The AFL he played the footy of chamomile ointment

He rubbed the passion, she remote the shovel for the pick handle
He drove the FJ Holden, a blemish from the days of old,
He pardoned a grape he sold, the lathered the ointment

TAMARA AND SHANE

He wielded an axe caught a shovel, he drove Tamara into oblivion
She wept the touch, the Iceman, she called him!
She drove the sty into a colonel of wheat, she stole the pig the stolen mice
She wilt the tissues a cause of sufferance,
A pledge to differ, hers was a well-orientated ordeal
She blew his spinach; she tried a hard time of it!
The work of Jason and the boys she parted a company of friends
A duo split her courtesy of act, a triumphant malady
She cornered Geoff, he doze the pants off, he fetish
The pride of the Australian Armed Forces with ray' she pardoned
A discreet melody, she wage a dollar of sixpenny recluse
Hers sympathetic to the least, she pride her rocking horse
Her domain the pride of family, a recluse she engendered the whisper of the wild
She went the restaurant La porch Etta, she raised a violet,
The boys they stole her away, Easy Pickens!
The dollar she drove, the Kate the best of mates, she whispered the sale

LEANNE AND PETER

A biker she shoveled the green, he dozed a Bull-eye-pass
He tattooed the singular for a girl of eyelash
She marveled the treatise, she cried India of fashion!
The bib's he laughed, the older brother he bet you the snake!
The dollar sign he partakes, the brew of two younger children,
The romance he stole the mandy of his lifetime
The biker rabid the smile, a footman he established
A mild, he swore like an English gent he barked
A spouse the youngest has not met me yet!
He dribbled the cotoneaster, he smiled the boys at Red-fern,
He laughed the girl he set to marriage, he stole her away
The house he bought the couple, he swing the days away
He drove a pickle of Arden, he wept the pathways, into the glen!
He pride the sir Excellency of Bishop, the run of the bloody familiar,
A differ to squirt the patronage, kind sir!

The girl he knew for 10 years, she paved the discreet, the pig of poke,
The wager she estranged the widow of biker, they ridicule, they acquired the salts
The Hells angels she bravadoes the tears, she wellness trodden

ANNETTE OF ELOPE

She begged a moment to differ, she swelter a tear of magnificence
And she borrowed the Duty-of-care
The shovel she spent a rhythm, she buried a quota of steam
The catapult, she Wedge-tailed the poor man succinct
Her violet pores of elegance, she laughed the show pony into a straight
The Pentecostal church she hungered at pains for him to come
She cried; please make a dummy for the bed!
The colonel of wheat, my little person feels the scrub of doctor
The lice have a feeling, she dove a cocktail of dusted fruit
The husband will not mind! She wrote voyeur of sympathies
Her treatise, what Nonsense! She laughed the smile of grace
She cried his love of affliction, she buried his loath
The lover laurelled, the stay she left

HAROLD AND RUBY

The ageless of home, the retirement home
He begged a Karen, suspended the negligee
He stowed the Ruby, a Sims of the village
He reaped the tired old misses, he cried Joan, better not!
She loaded his Chevrolet, the ladyship she raged an 80 year old
A cry baby she wept, a saloon bar they sailed
The oceans of bedlam, the fuse of the Sims
They met the family, the Keith a builder he spoke of the will
He cried do not give it to the children!
He barged the Lucifer' he paddock the supported ailment.
He forestalled the cabbage, ruby went to bed
And she cried Harold! She loaded a Bishop
And he parented the Port Arlington household
She dozed, the Sleep-out, a Peregrine Falcon

BIB'S AND MANDY

He drove the linen basket, he friendly a waver
A tear in the eye for the Shaman of France
His petal a rose of abundance, I shy-away!
The Mandy his girl, a girl he frolic's he salvo a retrofire
He ganged the greens, the house he nettled the pardon but its suppertime!
He did the rebuke to a woman he sold the sweet sherry and rice
A chicken noodle he befriended a man in the chair
He sold a runaway, he befuddled an ecstasy
He ramrod a pill down the Old digger's throat
He riddled the tears of Mandy
She said the dollar sign has made the sweep, the million is mine!
They docile a fed up trumpet of abuse, they ferried the little darlings
They stole the kitchen, the Val they smiled at the nonsense
The scholar of Fatima, they rode a sour, a ridicule made hers, she loved until dawn

ANTONY AND CLEOPATRA

A Cleopatra of niceties, she bellowed a tear
The Anthony of legions he buck a Cold-stream guard
A bullion of wheat he silo the grass
He loved the widow bent on esteem, he shadowed her currant demise
Awfully spoken hurrah, hurrah!
He drove her wild, the gangrenous smiles, the naivety of nature she love
The wattle bird sung, the throaty pith, she met the bird of song
The lerp the frog he growth the sum, a 1000 gold dinas
He shadowed her buck, the servant she killed the lice!
She roped the glamour, the turtle she fed
The steely eyed midget, the pug of recluse
She yearned the waver, the reeds she found
Promiscuous Valerie the tide republican
She pubic her scruff the violet she succumbed
The Mavis of doctrine she transcribed
A accord fortune in sloop she paid, the Marge of love'
The dream she doctored, a French kiss from a viper she cried

MICHAEL AND MANDY

The Michael he romanced the Mandy extremes
Of comfort, she drove the man into spittle
She wavered his doughnut the esteem of intellectual

The stream of tears they cried the house of no-consequence
They waver a frond, an alligator they spoke of
The swami they comfort the Dwight falls well spoken
They saw the coming, an antelope they rode

BOB FITZPATRICKS

They spoke wielding abstracts, the car and bikes
Bob run a circuit of specially tuned, the rally he collided
Driver laughed, I drove a specially tuned, a Datsun of fraud
The pilot of the airways, he left, he spun, around and around
He came back, the parents had beckoned, the board of lodging
He croaked a stubby; bob answered a pledge of iron
The spun of the wheel, the greasy garage mechanic
He spun the tire of groove, he pulled the piston, and he lodged the oil filter
Margaret his wife, she docile the genuine, she called the tea

GUADALCANAL

They sailed the reefs, the gun boats they trivial
The salts of piers, the moors they cried the alligator cove
The beaches, the gunfire riveted the shoals
The dummies they wade the beaches, they drilled the Gunfire
The posts they bullied those blessed, gunnery positions
The soldiers lay, they scurried the platforms, the diggers rampant
They harried the pulpit; the dispose of bullets whined
They boast of the nip, the Bonsai swords harried
They glittered in the light, the sun scalds the tenement
And they guile those bridges, the Gun-nests, and bridges
They harried, the flame throwers they pillaged the nests
The turtle said, my loss of culver the whip the ant cried as the blood spattered
The blood gnawed the holdouts, they locust they bleed
The slow reap across the shores, the entanglements whipped
The slow dying of species, the guns whipped the Harriet
The dove it shied the tender footing ashore
They mossier the whaler, they climbed, the tank he roared
Those Detroit diesels they encumbered a bitter remorse
The soldiers lead the ballast of Cold-hard-steel
They prod the tuckers gorge, the men of peak, their differences lay dead

JOHN AND ABIGAIL ADAMS

They reaped the cotton fields of Arizona, they vilified the fire
They built the confederacy up from scratch
They purveyed the nurture of olden times
They led the charge of oceans of union
The ranks they died, the squalid Richard, the old woman Abigail, she cried the Gray-coats
The Rebels do acquire a tenement, they fervor a talon of white blades
They cried an oath, win or loser remarks, and the blade of white death
A destitute native to the home soil
The Quincy Adams caught a flack under-siege
The wife Abigail she affronted a cage
Of nested Cherokee Indians found the rebels astounded
The badger rank nested the rested colonials
They savaged the duel, the revering quality, the Quincy he led the charge
Of rivers button, the furor alienates him, the stagnation of old
The Andy Stonewall' she flew the page, the old dreary legged wife
A John he savaged the fields with flossy Goldie
He tried the Wilfred, he glamour the pickers
He sold the blacks, a Bowie he flaunted the arrowhead
He beat the slaves, the Blue-coats they depraved the so long

THE D-DAY INVASION

The landing craft they drove the wedge, the soldiers whipped the array
They threw up, they blessed the crosses
The haven of riches they cloven the hoof
They prayed the iron, the rifles, their darkest hour, readied, the M16 carbine
The paratroopers they burdened the high wire
The bullet whined, the tracers they pledged
The knit grey wire, the oceans of multicolor
The Powder-flashes of gunfire, prone the flickered images
They landed an Under-fire they drove the iron curtain down
Blank the stray round, the blackness of 6am
They grounded the gliders, the landed the craft inland
The bridge they must take land until relieved!
The beaches they covered the blankets of blood
The scurry of fire, the entanglements they lager the fruits of despair
The hover of black bean sausage and sour kraut sauce
The blinding Vickers they peppered the wounded they lay-dead
Resolute the cowards they cried, crossed with blood-oaths

The blank of Richard, they bullet grazed the tower it billeted
The powder flashes, the burning of flickered bullets
They ran for cover, the prowess of gunners mate

BRIDGE OF REMAGEN

A rickety old bridge, war torn the bridge doth sail
The winds do whistle, the Nazis grey uniforms
They brew a stem gun he Germans the pot, the tanks of panzer they rival
They arrive, the bridge of Rummage, the bridge of remargen
The allies, the race for the bridge, the allied advance
On the stowage of cattle cross, they stew the girders, they set the charges
The high command says; blow the bridge, at a cost
Of the 9th advance, the allied armor corps, they billet
The dynamite bridged, the Nazis they fire the rounds
The jack of trout, he waters himself, the turtle he prides the leper steers the bedfellow
The natives play havoc, the barge of fears sails the river Rhine
The gunners of Nazi pride, the lemon of heft lieutenant gray
He settles the gray of girders, they blew the bridge, the allied advance
The tanks of allied, the cause of the Sherman tanks
The bitter GI's, they bilge the excitement gathers
The shear heights they strangle the bridge of remargen
The stem fires, a GI gets a round of stem betters
The cauldron of fire, the bridge it capitulates
The bridge stands despite the bomb

CLARA BELLE

A Lancaster of plight, the twin engine hornet
A plague of bombs dropped, the twilight guise
The motors roared a pattern of fire
Groped! a fanfare of maze, the chop of winds blew her off course
The tail, she wept a hail of gunfire
She drove the pepper of salted beef, she bewildered the stem
And! she bewildered the sentence
A wind blew the fervor of shouts, the tail end Charlie got his
The navigator caught a stray round, the twin belly gunner shot a puddle of blood
He flamed the cockpit stared a grimace, the Messerschmitt psalteries the aft
The plane pulled a gunfire shuddered, the cockpit rose abuse, hurrah
The engines they billeted the hornet, the bombardier he relinquished too
Of a hook, he dropped the bombs, he cried loss!
Those Germans of devil! They died!

He cried the radioman a sickened, distress signal waver the wing
Their opposite number, the wingman he caught the shrapnel
He quivered the fire, the Lancaster blew up!
He blew the winds of Hercules, the radio chattered

WOLF PACK

The sub capitulated, the screws it bent the rod of helm
The sailors wept the lightening of blue
The all-quiet, silent running, the captain Dervish he cried
The mood was a patronage, a yellow sailor cried
A seaman caught a flood; a broken back the skip caught a frigate
The crosshairs he whipped a duel
The frequent mister Jones, the executive officer
He sunk a brew, the frigate blew up!
The Morse code chattered a freeman belt
The radio officer he cried no more battle at bargain straits
A torpedo leapt tentative astern, the coxswain felt a murmur
The tide rushed in the vents, the still he broke the pass
The stern torpedo room rang a midget
The sub corkscrew, the bath he prepared at home
A despairing motive, a memory awakens the toil!
He cried his wife and kids, he dozed the coxswain asked
A call for the oil well, the bilges have a run dry!
He parched the drunk, the seaman Scott
The boson he laughed, the engines have spun

NO MAN'S LAND

The trenches lay deep aspire the mud of loathing, the slosh of boots
The jerry he tossed the pomegranate, he sped the halfwit
He dwindled the spread, the jam from home, he quit the séance
His belvedere the crypt, he drove the bayonet home
He cried the blade, the pocket of bull
The sphagnum moss in the dried up Harry
He dozed the old shed, he remembered the Peat moss
He drove the howitzer the bottom dollar
He bastard the old bullet it popped the heavy
He heaved the tyrant to pluggins of jerry the plug nickel
He spared the German, the Bosch he betrayed
The footy game they played, the madam butterfly they surrendered
With their pants on! They plagued the sherry of plump potato pie

The sponge of mud, the boots O' cavern, rapture they succumbed the needle

They paid homage across the trenches

Of spite, a mortar played havoc; the shell blew her teeth out

The dysentery they waist deep

Gunner, the sergeant's mate, he sped over the top

BISMARK

The battle of Bismarck Sea they cry

The swelter of arms, the difference of keel the ballast

They plagued those honorary seamen's plight

The dale of open voyage plagued

The pit of hull, the keep they died

The pleasant of surroundings, the deep of captain Bred-low Smith

He docile the smithereens, he scanned the wreckage

Oh ah the kingfishers had lain

The torpedo bombers streak! Hit the target, Dead eye dick!

They laid the harriers, they plummet the buoyant

The floozy of yachtsman, the heave boys', heave the guns that peat

The keel of martyrdom has blown her river of smite

The harrow seethed, the licorice broke, the boilers exploded

The tide of frivolous daemons of the sea

The gorgons myth of pass they died, away boys away they cried

ANTONY AND CLEOPATRA

They loved like love birds in the wind.

They cried, the swept of tears, acquired glances.

The Marcus Antonio's, he liver her pancreas

The motif forces the abandonment of Greek

The handmaiden slowed a pitch, she killed the maids

He docile the rubber swan she held, her courtesy she waned

The slave she pampered with a steely whip

She sarong her budgie she cried the asp

She boasts the negligee she didn't wear

She stole the love the patron saint of Hermes

She wandered the cow lick, the nettle brush, she staved

The violet a nuisance she depraved a boy, a womb she spent, an asp

A kin she so loved, a fetish of admiration she kept!

She wept the old sty of the Hebrew slaves

She wandered aimlessly through the encamp of ghetto

The slather of grief she portrayed the cat of nine tails
She drove the spike, harried the bosom she wed to marry
The golden change she drove a kennel, her pet dog Horus

PEARL HARBOUR

The planes they soared, the pendulum it crazed
The heights, the ocean boiled the seams of the craze
The Arizona broke the bastard cried out
The horses of the apocalypse' it hovered, the deepest ravines
The Jericho it flamed, the tail of a zero
The planes bombed the streets, the havoc gruel the steel whipped
The admiral of the camp, he riddled the midway island
They scout, two planes lofty wing tips, the criteria, the Alabama sunk two bombs
The Louisiana doubled the jack of stares, the coarse way it paddled the rim of fire
The navy of wartime it beached the tiger, the submarine recluse the tights
The destroyer plummet a jack of spades, the mess it blew a hole
Men's shorts, dressing gowns they caught unawares
The National disaster the Roosevelt cried
A travesty of whale proportions, they stowed the appeal, a tired old man
They shot the Jap planes, the doze of diggers they acclaimed
A footstool, a memorabilia of perturbed, the shrill of air raid sirens
The hospital took a bandit of shaped explosive
The welt of harbor, the sting of Jap bullets whined
The passage of planes they loaded

THE ZULU CAMPAIGN

The generals of the armchair, defeatist smiles
Their Zulu bedlam of badlands reprised
They shook the tears, the island Uganda
Chief of the Zulus, he laughed the black sheep
He killed one of his people; they, the British spoilt the haven
Of riches, a cup of tea, a game of croquet, they stole the envelope
The lord Chelmsford he reaped the jacket for dinner he sped, the envelope
He drove a needle; those hypocritical Zulus must be taught!
To yield, they stole the land!
The dozer of spring salts, a war command is imminent
He vital the blood soaked pen!
He drove the dove to the chief, he frightened the chief
The British have apathy of struggle
The mule, we insist you lay back!

He dove the support, he clamored aboard his mount
He bet you a robber of clowns, a sweet sherry
He clover the fields, the British crossed the river
They wiped a colloquial surrender, the terms of battle-hardened troops

JACK AND PAM CROSSWAITE

They Herby the caravan park of Dyeline
The rebel they sailed the Port Phillip Bay
The strong man of the pacific they cried
Old Pam laughed a sixpence, she cried her boyfriend Harold
She added the Sea has its victims, assault pier
The permissive husband cried she rigid the bow,
The tornado struck a company of fray
He fought the war in the Sea of utopian Japan
Beseech me now, the wild bull, champagne flowed!
They won the war, peddled the boats, he drove the wedge,
The pocket halfpenny bride he fell in love
Skipper! The dog of the Floats they played poker
With a drum of beer, the Xmas party they gathered around
The smiths they brew, the Kentucky-red-eye
They drunkard the swills, the Aubrey Boathouse
A Christmas party, the blight of vigil, the peak
The kids they drove the whaler, undersea with Sam
The yellow submarine, drowned his boat every Easter
He sailed a tall fighting clipper, the sloop old Freddie's dream lost her keel
Old Harold bet you, a steel mule, cross Waits they crowed
A wagon of spite, the boy he took on old Jack

THE ALLPORTS

Old Herb his wrecking yard, the Brougham of leach
He peddled the squat, he belched the grapper drink
He stole the wood his latest boat, endeavour he levied the misses
He waver the rescue the boys he drove the wooden he simmer
The Alan and Geoff, he riddled the plank, he played the golf old grey Jack
He labored the rebel the boat with as many feuds to her name
He strode the Dyeline residence with the Gut ridges of ownership
He pardoned the Boatshed, they peddled the grog, the mice they laughed, the Roulette-wheel
The jingles they played, the pavement rattled
The ordeal, the ski boat he through a gear
Old Harold fixed the spinnaker; he drove the misses M14 Sea-lady

And he shouldered the penny sixpence, the navy frigate
He came the southern part of Italy, the war he salvaged the pity
The Mussolini he hated with envy,
The spokes of the dreamboat Mrs. Ely, he sailed the golden wares, the fishes he saw
The blight of jack, the Pam he boast the old lady she swum, she bent the liquor
The old sea-witch, the Jet impoverished it at pains, the surrender
The Sea-lady came to ground; The shallows she caught the shallow deck

HERB AND ANN

He drove the Smidgens, the whaler, the tramp of pots;
He traded the scallop for a seaman
A ketch he paddled the ocean, the channel he wept
The whale of a time he sped, the allsorts special,
The brougham he loved', he wept a well spent penny
The sugar he fed the cow a dumpling, he stoked the carpenter to fix the keel
He dove the silver rainbow of tides, the king tide they brawl,
The snapper point of recluse he stowed to crippled sub
The buccaneer of ship, the sideways sloop he engendered
The wafer of deep-sea core, he stole the 80 foot hole
The backbone of the freighter, the nuisance dam thing, it weight the chime
The engine blew a rod, the sump of bilge it cracked the pledge
They pulled it from the water, snapped the Rochester timing gear
The jack laughed old rebel of seamen pledge
They rode the Cole pepper they marched the rebel homewards
The steamer they weighed the dummy to a fly caster wheel
They cast a rod the deep black hole, the channel arrested the toll

KEN AND MARGERET

Ken he dove, the flight of a pigeon,
The aero model lethargic the Royce of rolls
He grimaced a wedded flight of passion
He fled the boys', he drove an eagle in flight
The Margaret he loathed the special, she studied the bachelor of ministry
Her wedlock the child, her third born a crook
Of steer, the antelope she fled, a buttered sandwich on bread
A roll for the honeymoon, she stared the odd bloke
She stayed the honeymoon quarters and she raved the skeptic of pleasantries
She stood the kids' the wedlock chapel of remembrance
She stole the affections of older brother

She whispered cute sayings, the ken he wanted a heavenly greeting
He wavered the boys' he whispered the chapel
He labored the Scottish of prejudice

MICHAEL AND MANDY

A Michael bled for his wife, the three kids' he bled
The passion of instinct, he brother the Silverado, the mine of self surrender
They waver a duel of lovers' quarrel, they fell the loss from grace'
The ocean of dreams they befell the rogue of settle
The hammer of ninja, the turtle he wax
The felt ribbon tied a ruse, she wept his pen
He instinct the grace', she Wendell the rose, a Freemason's paradise
The curb of linear suggestive acts of diplomacy,
She cried he broke into tears
He scabbards the friendly notion of his, not hers!
He thrilled the personage of well driven spite
He drove her paper tiger into submission
She clouted the dog! She rough and ready the movement of Opera
She laughed the silken web of deception
He smiled his Pet, the Kids of borne the upheaval
His jury of the arrears, he swooned

MICHAEL AND JUNEY

The wedded couple they laid a grace of flame
The warmth they moved a platform, the singer of the Grand opera
The stage of lights the pivot they stopped the show,
The raison loaf June she laughed
The Scots pride she remised the vigil
The lovely nightingale she speak of freedom a pledge
The Wings of harpsichord, the mellow they depraved
The widow of horn, the crime of door chime
The cousin of Nut bush he claimed a fiber of dried the sultanas
He Besieger her not, the harriet of talent, he couldn't play
The rheumatism he forthright a fellow of grasp the tear
The play of act, the one course play, the open valley, the spirits they soared
The Glendale of speakers, the marshal of amplifier
They rode the rose, they cabbage the orchestration
A Valerie of singers pause, the singers were very indisposed,

The twilight of melody, the pause in remission, the stringed quartet
They cried the season, a bust the girl, surprised the Quartet!
The bassoon of talent, the cupboard bare they strung, I moved

THE CURIES

Michael and Mary she rode stout, scientists of the mount
The Royal Geographical study of Americas
The pastors of the holy Christian church, the devout of furnish
They fixated the penicillin, they made a straw standup
They vilified the Radon, the cup of tea they dreamt
They learned the fission of a tea cup
They saw dancing girls, a dream they ferment
The glossy whites, the snow blankets, a malady of breezes
The esteemed summer's day, the couch they slept a notepad
The brim of the sugar turned sour
The crust on the bottled milk, the pink tissue of matron
And the soup glazed a pocket, a remedy sours the soup
The glow of the radioactive turpentine they glad, and the waist of the broth
They soured; Iodine dry the kerchief of silken
I moved the radio it bumped, and the sugar fell
The glut of bowl the Radon glowed

ABELARD AND HELOISE

A nun of Heloise she abode the sanction, a message in a bottle
A pond for Elphonse, the Abelard a scholar of repeated attempts
He wrote a letter, the love' of her heart
He wrote, a dear Heloise my love' of twice profound
A built, the interest my scorn as profound I seek
The squalor my knees I drooped, the schemes of profound
The need I fulfill the barter, the nun of my dreams,
The girl Heloise she drooped the vain swan
An aura the interest, my maid misses Honeysuckle
A tease the sheep, the drought I feel the anguish of Romany
The loved' I bequest the need silver blend
The brooch of Fatima, a lady's kosher
I beseech ye now, I lovers breast, the columbine of fresh milk
The wound I do know of you signed the lover

ANNIE AND FRANK BUTLER

The Oakley hall of fame, the frank butler she sold a buckaroo
She slaved a Petri dish, defamed her midget
A potshot of ball, she pilled the musketeer
She traveled the circus of fame, the wild Bill Hickok
She drove a pet snake, she whimpered the soldier
A square eye view, he sold her into a pocket, a touch she fell the love'
A man she reaped, a marksman of eyed shot the puss
He broke her mount; he beheld the round tail of sheep
Herding, the buffalo they mark the muskrat
The feel of 45 calibers they square the violet
The town they painted blue, the docile sheriff he run
Muck, he claimed old Annie a show girl, he Wurlitzer's the tide of grief
The girls they played the piano, the saloon of barkeep

THE BUCKBOARD AND CALAMITY

The calamity of breezes, she shot a pot black
Naked in a rainstorm, she harrowed the defeatist smile
She laughed Billy the kid into oblivion
She scouted a plea, and the union wept her estranged widow
She laughed the Dirt-water-fox, she loved' a firm grasp on reality
She tested the buck, the Indian, she harried the jumbuck
The ply of the old fool, she resolute the young soldier
He shot the Lampoon that craved his sympathy
She docile the Jess of gunfight, the days of old
She laughed the whiskey; she laughed the frontiersman, Grizzly Adams
She pancake the butter on the old mule her keepsakes
They laid her to waist, the buckboard they cried
Calamity cried, a drunkard thirst her ale of Dependence
She mulled the owl hoot that raped the towel
She shot the Sundance kid, he borrowed her butt
He short order the cook on barrel of rice
He shot the limey coward that called her man

EVA AND ADOLF

The Adolph of Nazi Germany, the plague all
The charismatic he duo, he rasp the pig of geriatric
The Albert spire he diligent the fields of glory
They played the women, a cat fight developed

They stray the pigeon of velvet streets they sour the Stream, the cove so near
The arousal of depth a deep thought of scowl, they played the horn
A depth of dying, fulfils thy independent thought cried Adolph
A needle and cotton, the dregs they hornet the needle
A fiber they chased, the chastise they plagued the generals
The hornets nest, the needle of women they chastised
The grub, the steely-eyed visionary
The charisma they rebuked the tide, the mistletoe they surmised
The allegro of symphony they plagued deep ruse
The midst rolled deep the skirt, the steely Eyes they welled
The Rochester, the locust plague, the Lugar they hornet, the grub they bite
The deep astound the parrot of cheesy smiles
The sweltered the deep the acquired love, the sexual connotations
The grub of pantheons, a closet they steep
The women of sleek and mild they docile

QUEEN VICTORIA AND THE PRINCE

She maid a patron saint' a vicar she tidied
He quirk her dinner her snuff he peddled
He acquired the salt of vicar, he chastised her bed linen
He broke a tear, the salt of Peter, the glory box
The snuff of lid and compacter of women ointment
And rub the gentle dowry of genuine salts
The face she promenade, the guilt esteemed edge, love harrowed
The affliction of tastes, she buried his face
The Albert of prince, the leper of frog
A timeless gent, he beleaguered the frog
She smelt a Disraeli of impetuous
He lend her maligned sympathies of touch
A weave she shook as the chipmunk entered the room
A Dahlia roses she roasted the nuts
The Albert swept him away, he closed
The daughter he apprised, the Queen Anne her featureless butt rose
He hampered the picnic rug, the Joy of becoming
A steward grasps the meadows, the secret garden
The child' plays the palsy of notoriety
He plays the weave, old English gents, and the aristocracy of England
She moved old Albert the boat to china
The liquor cabinet my dear Albert
The crystalline jelly for the gout my pardon
The cheese from the pantry, take the servants out to be blinded

They stoked the fire over, they basked
The fruit to the cellars fetch the fetish
Farce those servants to my living quarters!

DARNIE AND CORRESPONDANT

A darnie of the kids, the woman acquired tastes
An interest; she mounted a firm grasp on the dollar
She wrote a pigeon, the hole he narrowed
The special of clamor she pardoned his matter
He minded her childish play, a horseless carriage
She mute and the devy girl of reckless ambition
She mule a playhouse, she straddled the farmer
The Ozamis City she played a diligent memoir
She asked an I-pod she developed a no-leave nor say
A sensory of childish ambition, a deprivation, and a depth of play
The ordinary the pumpkin patch she appealed the lover's permit
A man is my boss, you are head of the family
May I have permission to leave the hallowed footsteps of victory!
She repealed the ocean, a sing song, a Hip Hop she danced the rhythm
She admonished, the sense to which borrowed an appeal to be loved'
The earnest of darnie she played the rocking horse
The woman of the gaunt, a Filipino she dragged

DAME NELLIE AND CHARLES ARMSTRONG

The Charles and Nellie she wept, the showgirl of talent
The father clandestine her works as a lady
A soprano and her understudy, the Christian ladyship choir
She gained notoriety at the college of the Arts,
She studied the opera; she felt a grasp of Kelly Colquhoun
And she wrote a script, she sold her mother into the weatherproof
She starred the musical lovers of saint' Lawrence
A Petersburg she florist, she ran a ladies corset of finery
The upper class she docile a scheme of things of red Blackwood,
The furs laid her in waiting, she cried Charles Lindbergh Smith
She dallied the Diary of Anne Frank
She junior the peasant to the late Charles Armstrong
She married the come a cropper the olden days
She sped the nickel Cobram of spite, the sprig of nectar ointment
She sung soprano of the league of English gents
She spite the negligee over the table

She wrote the plans over Sydney Myer
The blue shade the tears, the significance, the shapely abundance
The plans of Melbourne, the Mayor made her, the Armstrong falls, she named

THE STRIP CLUB

A fantasy of Lovers quarrel, they vent their horror
They discord their parable as they meet
They bask the laurels of overture
They cry out dismay at the girdle, the audience cries
The onerous of R rated Clubs, X shops, Strip tease
They plummet the guise, they horrific the Constabulary
The Men of LeChic's, the Venue of paradise Hilton
They cry the tears; they strip the Arden of reproof settlement
They skip the repertoire of grouse
The fashion boutique, the Somersby Hilton Hats
The silken underwear, the silver of bras
They court the parlor, they slinky the overcoats
The marvel the gross iniquity of constituency glamour
They bless the Contuse the blessings,
They discreet the Crime, the insignificant

THE MILLIONAIRE AND THE DOVE

The Multi millionaire he is startled by the friar
He raved the dove, he acquired notoriety
The friar laughed, a billion of notoriety
He cried, the Billion the motion of Commodities
The trade of Fore X, the notice of foreclosure
The Dove laughed, a symphony of distrust
He acquired the Dell Jones; he drove the Dow, the Kerry
He overseas the trade, he cried, the motto of estrange
The goods of my nurture of pink, the disclosure of render
The furthermost of directory, the Rage of a bullish market
The thrive of stocks of commonwealth bullion
The thrive of monies spent well worth, the seasons of impoverished notions
The Dove aspired the Greek a curtail, she martini the aspirations of grub, her monies
She worked the fruitier of golden season, the furniture
A paradox of nuisance, a purveyor of State-savings-bank
Of china, the money-box grub, the seer of forex
Of men, she laughed the boyfriend, she corralled the petty allowance

The Spaniard for a spent pound, a quid too absorbent
A plug nickel too share, the pricing of a bag of Potato-chips
The mellow array of silverware, the petty money box

THE JOLLY ROGER

The flag of the empire Constantinople, he Cried
The sea worthy wench, the skull and cross bones of black flag
The plague of Hangman's noose, he cried
The bones of Cavalier, the rasp of lice, the skull of the ancestors pride
The blue beard ensign of piracy
The flagship of the Fleet, the Conclave of ships squalid
The bravado of remittance, he Galleon the rite
The Constantine of noble, the Romany of Guard
The poor old Oarsmen, they partake in the ruin
Of Sailor's whimper, she cried the master of the skip

THE FOXES LAIR

They grub the steely-eyed worshipper of the Clan
The Chancellor Adolph Hitler, the fiercesome blight
The growth on the side of his head, his madness broke free
A Himmler beckons the Albert spire, fanatics! he cries
The Velvet, the strong he bitter they cry!
The primrose steak, the zeal they motif!
The muse has legs to see, I relish my guilt pride, the languished!
I settle my allowances, they bomb with 1000 pounders!
I bomb their cities, the bi polar, I erectus!
The sham of needle erectus statutes, the privilege shalt die!
My presumption, the Jewish head of state, Rats the plague!
The charisma flows, ecstasy of parable I speak
Of a bemuse the temperament gathers a league of injust persecution
The Just of operation, the barbarous they flirt dirty the swerve
They mix the tears of righteous allowances, they grizzle the wire
The invasion of D-day they plot the enigma
They twain the Robust of glorious Adolph, the fiend
The sanctimonious, the partake, the mood!
In appreciable servants of the said prince I save the catholic
I boast nonesuch Ideals, I scorch earth, the debacle of sentence
The mere frogs of dubloon, I render the tears, the seas I succeed

THE BARGE OF LOUISIANNA

The paddle of waters, they strait the rivers Missouri river barge
They glove the gentleman's Cuff, they stout the Casino of death, butte
They stove the southern gentleman's Cove, they laughed
The prize, the grim wheeler they cry!
The patronage of ladyship's finery, the establishment rebuttal curve
They waver the cuff, the gentleman's epitaph
The waver for a spade, up the sleeve!
The paddle made a swish, swash, the wheel it became
The New Orleans they conclave the Captain of Louisiana preyed
A keen eye on that bottle of vermouth he stirred
The Plymouth Rock has ridden her bow they cried
The Soak of spoils, the Clydesdale of sidewalk, the Catwalk of stroll
They fermented a brewer's ale, the Ketch they levied the marshal
A toll of $ 5000 in bullion to the Confederacy they ferment the navy
The stole-way of purpose, they delivered a bounty, the Ketch it splayed a reward
The gun it revealed a motif, the knife an implement of terror
The slash and run! His grotesque, the heathen caught a round
The Gentleman asked of stow the Cargo
My delightful of Growth, the Seamen of quarter deck
A hound of skipper, he embodied the stout skipper
He cried the barrel of the finest port, the onerous of the old tug

THE OVERTURE

He basked the Theatre, a quagmire of resplendent virtues
The plague of drum set kit, notes of the express, the guitars string
The chorus of bland, oh the music of uproar, twice profound the harmony
The Oceans betwixt the harmony they do despair
They Grove the remembrances of pity
The Regent martyrs the Rabble, they stare, a Glim passage of time
The Circular abundance, the bassoon it labyrinth measure
Passing shadows in the night, awareness of life
The Monsieur of delinquent feathers
E' strums the orchestra plays, the final encore,
They brilliant, the butterfly scorns, resounds the reverb, excitement thrills
The actuation of drums, the bongo of the well tuned drums

RIO DE JAINERO

They slewed the streets of Rio, they pompous mute dressed in a fig
They robe the Clown, the Dais throne the spider leaped
The Oscar of giant, they paraded the Concourse
The wickedness blending the colors gave chase, the multicolor dwarf
They chased the bull; the goats cried the entourage raged
The whisper, the dancing girls, they whispered kiss me!
The Oak of timber branches they wilted
They Soccer the old Grasshopper, the gay of Mardi gras
They welt the Strawberry, contuse of vibrant, color interwoven
They latter day the reap, the multicolor of Verse
They sing, they strong-arm, and the Aztec Indians bore witness
They grotesque, the tired dance, a free for all
Cried the Dance, the fairies they paraded they kiss

THE TRENCH

They lay the trenches under foot, the malevolent, flailed in the Mud
They bartered the ordeal, they basted the Crows foot
Unbroken! They sloshed the Core, the Depths of the trench
The steely eyed myth over the broken maze of trenches
They billeted Rain dog down a Rabbits burrow
They cried the mesmerizing of decapitator, they slung
The whimper of lead lined boots, the Willowed the jack of the Hun
They sour the speckled the bullets, riddled the armor of squirt,
They patched a Grill, a periscope, they pancake the wire of entangle
They ridiculed the Boston, the red socks they billet
A trench of a game, passé the river of mud
A Hung the wild oats, cat of strap the bootie
The boot levied to Hun, the boast the old man sergeant of smites
The pie eyed Hun, he glorified the snap-shot

THE BEAR

He laughed the passage of Gravy
The mammoth Kaleidoscope of fluff
The cotton balls my lovely!
He waver a solace, the tuft of growth, and the claws they clung
And the grizzly metaphor of drunken the swayback
He shot the Frontiersman, he swayback the whaler
Esteem the way past, the cylindrical of bear

He shod the feel, he Babcock the brown he Cried

The cubs, the Darkness Creed,

The Oceans of fur, they glint testimony

Of rub, the docile hound, the buck he Clydesdale the Doe

A sheepish fern, the terror of Claw, the bilge of rascal

THE BARBER

He spike the Hair, he Do a Hair cut of smiles

A crew he cut the Shepard's Mix

He laughed the footless had the perplexed

He Ran the builder, he coaxed the bull, down

The Street, the barber of Colossus laughed

A Fixture on the wall, No Greenies allowed!

He bastard the old Bull wit a Cross of wedge top

The valor had passed away, he praised, he cross a dog

The hair a Bullish, the perm, a bull wave, he cut the army Cut

He spot the hydro, he Cow licked the perm

The shoddy blow wave

The barber the strap the Cut throat the razor, he scraped

A foul ball the TV Cried, an open Display of nerve

WANGARATTA

They Drove the Goulburn 'bloody' Valley highway

A Skip they abhorred, they cried the Buses driven, the driver called

They dough the silver bouquet, the tourists they plagued ruin

They diversified they wild the Stored of pawn

They bridled the stores, the rifle of Aussie-disposals

They enlighten the establishment, the Wood iron restaurant

Stove of Glances! He broke the china of the pot belly stove

They rivaled the passage west, the tourist bus

The driver called the National monument, the settlement greytown

The publican of Gary Paterson, the shearer

The pizzas the eagle brothers laughed

They Curio the pots of Deidre's palace of wares

The bus driver roamed, a quirk, the beer flows

They Clive the bully's hairdresser

The butcher the drill haven square gardens

The wineries beset El Dorado, the falls Creek of ski

They bask the golden waters, the heights, they cradled

THE SHIRLEE

He waged a fiddle, a Chime in a China box
He swayed swag, the billabong he lodged a penny grateful
A pooch, he laughed, a Matilda of sixpence agenda
He found a frilly negligee, he Swag a penny brook
He tired a lonely ketch
He bellowed the wine, he Cross the pooch
The porch he sank, the dog, a kelpie he laughed
The bronze whaler, he perceived the Crock
He whaled the Billy, and he found a Kitten
He followed the Matilda, the eerie eyed puss
The inlet to the local, the purse he followed
The pride of the uJack-rat, the puss followed

THE GHOST OF EMILY JANE

Emily frank an illusory of personage the ghost laughed
A spent rhythm, she aspired, the sea she painted
The Bow she strung, sweep the carpet, she cleaned
An elderly swayback, a Peter of Sail of antiquity soiled
The mellowing sea serpent, aroused her soul
She sold her soul, the river boat Captain, the ghost
The seas she plummeted, a Grace of torrent
A Benedictine, a grubber she cliché
She gout the town, heralds of sympathetic
A boarding room for ladies humor
She spelt the Licorice tide; she smelt the liquor of abundance
A Corkscrew; she tired the old Sea Captain, he came to visit

THE ACROBAT

He strove the Circus, the Act a Columbus
A sideshow act, the Stadium, a circus act
The Contortionist of plea, the rope to bargain
He barge the Stirrup, the horses they drew
A somersault, the flip of slide, the Jack of spades, the clown
They plague the ripe, those rose of petals, the snowman's plight
The showmanship the letter, they thrived the Lotus, a bird on a wire
The jeopardy of act, the tight rope on a wire
A high wire, they raced the arena, agenda warrant a Tidy

A BRILLIANT MIND

He swooped the Current of demise, he cried the Codex
The stillness he count the numbers he sour the Grand Scheme
He Cried, the Leo Morse, he Grandiose the last Verse
He trivialized the perplex glimmer, the encryption device
He laughed, the blonde caricature, the secretary he remorse
He Crowed the X= a1; he laughed the Code
The enigma Code, the war of the sea wolves
The battle of the Atlantic shoals, the wild typists dreams
The Silver-dove his Glad tidings, he watched as it perched
The whaler he pursued, the sea wolves, the tank he dreamt
The ocean of Drama, tears that spoilt their remorseless pattern
A solace they Screw the mind of Tully the capacitor
They matter the facade, the perilous numbers, the paper tiger

THE BALLERINA

She swept a tear, a flossy white dress
She spread the tips of her feet
Of mice a lay about, the pretty eve
The heels her lingerie, she flowed a Spartan of grace
The parity she floss, she Cried, the motionless
Of needless to say, the Dance
It portrays, the eagle of swans set the pillage
Of Tchaikovsky he plummet the wonder, she drove
Her little Frame, she spoke, the Swan Cried a league
The Vermouth tucked astray, the hoofs of the Deer

HOWARD HUGHES

He rasped the Fool of Spruce Goose
The plane of swim, e' laughed the Vegas saloon
He promoted the Empire of Silver, he bet the Craps,
The table of Swan, he played the fool
The resonance he depicted, the Outlaw of Mob
He laughed the Martin of *Oceans eleven*
He cried Sammy Davies, the junior, the labor of Love,
He Criminal the slather, a whiskey and cola, the bourbon he sacrificed,
He broke the depression, the men he worked, the aircraft Company
He stole the Underworld, the Vegas hotel
He Financier's the John F Kennedy before they shot his Debt

He staved the Golden rings hotel, he broke the chain
The ice pick he sought, the meadow of Nixon Watergate Trial
He expunged, he cried the Senator Waterhouse

THE SALOON

He Raised a Jack of spades, they laughed, and you cheated!
They shot the holes of jeopardy, the cantankerous of Come up pence
They cried, a whiskey shot O' Dear, the bourbon has ran dry
The Yellow dog saloon; the Deputy laughed
A Coke of rubber sack, the wood of burner
The fire place staunch the rabid, the fighting started a Raunchy
The saddle bounced as a Horseman rode, the Cattle into town,
The beech wood grove settled,
The marble of stature, the old rider be startled the fervor
They encroached the season, the poker hand, drew a flush and pairs,
They shot the man down in the midst of a dream

THE REVENGE

A Confucian Emperor says, the Ninja the warlord leaded
The sacred bond, the Samurai blend, the silken black he shed a gender
As he strings the bow, the cross he members, the arrowhead,
The blood the bedfellows, the lady of verse, she willows the nurture
The Robe of Japan, the Chinaman erupts a verse
He Cries, the woman of his Dreams assassinated by ninja

THE WIZARD

He Cried the Saturn of Stars, Saturn ate his mother Jupiter
He crazed the orphan Ulysses
The stolen the Hercules amulet, His Crazed Zeus, the Father of the planets
The Grove of Spinnaker, the Odious sailed the Tall Dragoon, the sailing ship Ephesus
The timber wolf raved, the Prometheus legend of Pluto;
Pluto the legendary ogre, wept for his mother saturn
He crowed the genie of the lamp, he forsake the old
He politely added the Gorgons of old, the banshee stole her mistress
And he beckoned the wild nimrod settled the score
He welded the matterhorn of pegasus, she crowed the pony of delight

THE MIRACLE ON 57TH STREET

A Santa of mementos, he crazed the web of security
A Kris Cringle he blatant, a reindeer, he cried a Sufferance
Of honorary spite, he plagued the Courts
And he roused the sleigh, he worked at Macys
He cried the Working man's Idol, and he cried the young of Detroit
His Car the Jack in the box, he gave the snowman of capri
He sue the Post office, the enormous at odds
He preyed the bismuth surrounds, they put a psychiatrist to Work
He dreary Disney of burden, they stroked the love of Greatness
He climbed the magical array of Snowman's boots,
He sleigh a reindeer, he Cried Rudolf, Prance, and vixen
The Rest of his Deer he laughed, a boot of snow,
He relic the Russian philanthropist, he barter the wealth
The Open Fair ground, he sold his Wares

BOULEVARD OF LIGHTS

They satire the nights of the Boulevard
The Toorak of Settled, they robed the Carols
They gross the pigeons, roof top they rebuke
The Santa of reindeer, the peruse the driven niceties
The Séance the young Cry out, the abundance, the tears they bilge
The electrified wonder, the blues, tinges of yellows lit
The abundance foils of Street huskers,
They shadowed the myth; they stole the Virtue of Christmas
They laughed the parents of 1000s,
They patron the Arts, they cry abundance
Corkscrew the wine of Champagne Delight
The roof top splendor, the serenade, they billet the carols
The Sadness of family's course, they drive the Cars
The parks of Boulevard Crossing

DESERT

The Armed Forces they pillaged, the desert sands of Mildura
The bright Oranges, turquoise, Greens, they blemished
They drove the hafeus corpus; they vilified the sands of Oyeon
The little desert of Mildura, blemishes, they random the Hutchie
They blight the snowman, the permitted a direct assault
The winds blew, the Ardent of pillage of rifles and muscetele

The nightmare of Dunes, the desert sands whipped
The dreary legged old mule, they proposed the anguish, the route march
The desert sands, the dusk of Fervor, they cried the water Bottles, a sip at a time, a dry
The Helicopters they chopper relief of barnacle
They shed the night time of Bulls rush, they Shepard the morn, as the cock crows
They built the showers of bush turkey
They cleaned the Bren Guns, dust of bloody tyrant

THE GALA BALL

They shined the finery, the women they spoilt
They swallow the Kate brush, the fiddle they muse
They polite the spoil, they shone the purple, the negligee
They purposed the imminent, they bask
The finery they masked a yellow façade
The autumn of growth, the grotesque scenic abundance
They cried, the autumn dew, they Vat 59, they perused
The shadows of springtime, the verbose of character
Endearing, bequeathed the shadows of torrent the nearsighted
The plum, the blossom of culture, the bosoms they spay

ARMEDEUSS

The Mozart of the sixth Symphony, the Amadeus the musical affidavit
The fiend he boast, the city glen, the ladies he broke, a snuff
The opie he cherished, the Redwood of galloping Bonaparte, he bothered
The Halls of grace, Fame a legion of terror, the Cry of the patronage
He broke the will of Beethoven, the String Quartet, the deliverance
The Piano Concerto he played, the Orchestra, a Violin, a flute, a malady of string
A gaze of harpsichord he robed, the Strings of Bow, he lecherous
A Mother of Violet array, applause he sought, he cried allegiance
He Flock the butterfly, he belched the Harmonic,
The dutiful array of sound, come alive,
He Stout the Court of Louie the third
He played a Conductor, the Bolshevik of sound
He saw the Quartet, he played the bassoon, he crowed the implement
A Tea he snuff, he belch the winged trumpet
Of fluted the expression, the China he played

THE MUTINEER

He barge the purple Nightingale, he roved the Spanish Galleon
A Wager torn for a Leg iron,
He launched a boat the horn blower yelled, a mister Christenson he cried
The Stackhouse of the Wood Pickens the Dread of the oceans ferment
He Said, the permit of doctrine, thy swindle of pancreas
He fermented the pew, the Dread the high seas
He dowse the spinnaker, he Colonel the mates over the pike
He delivered, but how could they tell!
The mattress of have Shaw, e' drank the Spanish regime
The skipper mister blower, the master of pioneer
The thread of belief, the childish play, the masts do have
He Stack the rat hole, he prevalent the mister
His Galleon the sentence, he blew the wild forties of pillage
The galloping tides, he famished the old tug of galleon, and he stole the wager
The Crew laughed the old peg leg, he whaler the West Indies
He plagues the haul of keel, the survivors, do saturate, the scurrying leaves
He Stowed the Stomach, the bitter of a Keg

THE GARBO

He raved the Garbage truck, the Council at Arms men,
He wasted no time, a six am Start
They woeful the expectant bobby, the boss
They rallied the Streets of bishop, a vicarage of alcohol
They acquired the terms, the Cans of Victoria bitter
Flagon the mite, the terrorist plague,
They threw the Garbage premise, chased the leathers
They bilge the waste, they derelict the Farm of Scoundrel,
Bloat a Cold stubby of Victoria Bitter, a Beer for the thirst
A Rummy staggered, he Bloke the boys, he rode the back,
The Ute of Spanish Dump truck he famished the Cold one, he ripe the truck
The Rip e' embraced the pit street picnic
The baker street boys languished the crime
The Council Decreed the 4am Start, they all went to the pub
They stout a brewery, they clover the back street,
The parlor of Officers, the mess they regimented the squat

THE WHITE COLLAR

He belted the Keyboard, he rose
The open printer and he blemished the Girl
He Tare the gross, iniquity of paperwork
The boss shouted, no Grace! He Thumbelina,
The Crack in the wall, he studied the woeful,
Degenerate of Hard drives, he ambition the curve
He snuck the smoke; he bridled a bit of whiskey and Cola,
A nip of brandy for lunch, a bouban he squalor
The boss ordered an Overrun of paper,
A paper trail he Wentworth the ladies
He Screw the secretary, he laughed the bundle of flora
He abundance the messages, the memoirs he Roped
He caught the fat lady, he called the whore

CHECKPOINT CHARLIE

They broke the wall, they chased the Harriet
The Checkpoint Charlie and the Americans
They Cried, the Berlin wall, they belvedere the Rifles
They rasped the scale, the Wall
They billeted the kosher, the Soldiers Guard
The Grape, they fired a round, and they platoon,
The Station of East and west, north of picket line
They blow a hole anything that moves
The gripe the Snowman pillages, they stow the frightened Russians
They vilify the Rosewood Gun posts
They burrowed the iron curtain; Deep the forthright wall

THE BLOSSOM

They bud the refreshing, the bees of lard hark, hark
The Lander flies, oh scrape, the Signoras of flamed of uproar
Scatter's the wild, flurry of winds blown
The scenic shrubbery, the loaf of inflorescence they clove
Arbor, the poise of fruition, and the seeds they do scatter
Preponderance, the glitter of plague of Florence
The spectacle harbors, a Pea of Refreshing, the needle oh spouse thee
The leaf of abundance pleasure the ripe midst
They swallow the shallow, the fernery catacombs
The Cat like breezes, they wind blown ecstasy,

Of Caricature great and small, the innermost of tears
The flatulent Depiction mellows the flowering enigma ripens
The seed of Zealous frightens the yellows of fears
The desolate fawns, the dusk,
Harsh of old pepper, the hues of floral,
And the abundance of shaped mosaics, the fernery scatters
The birds of sap drawn, the kingfisher envelopes

THE BUTTERFLY

A pupae of old, the Grub of thistle of Birchwood
A woeful sight, he shines the Caterpillar, a multicolor dwarf
In the pigeon coop, the slaughter of possum lose
The dwarf, he Grimaces the Virgin, the steely eyed moth
He cries the mellow, the Cocoon he mellows, and he crawls the leaf
The Strawberry he assumes a Growth
He Bicentennial the liquor
He cries the moth; the flies endanger the moth of extremities
The silver eye virgin, he envelopes the patch
The leaf he slimes, he barbarous the tiny allegro
He beckons the Star of shapes, the willow of shadowy moonlight,
He Cross the Ovum of Turtle dove

THE OWL

He Hooligan is the privy, a nocturnal of beasts
Catlike instincts, he burrows the finite recourses
He Cries a Hoot at night, the proliferation of a bat, he buries the felt
He cries the one eyed owl, he Barbaric,
He acclimate the rabbit, he talon the thirst
A grub he Wastes, he cries a Hornets nest
He Frolics the neighbor of Bat, he prolific the nearsighted Dwarf
He buries the meadow, he nests the trees, he shadows the ringtail possum
He bewilders trust, the Organ of sympathy flight

THE CROCODILE

The Log of astray, a Calamity in pursuance
The well orientated reptile, stronghold, the floating barge of meat
The profanity of the wild, the wood dwarfs the upheaval
And the marshes beheld the undercurrent, the flame of abhorrent

The torrent of the deep, the moat of drowned sloth,
Of patronage, The fiber of derelict
The ocean of Credence, the felt good of marshes
The Robin red breast sleeked overhead,
The crocodile snapped, the mongrel caught a beaver
The wave of stem to stern, reaped danger, the Crocodile rolled itself over
The snap over powerful jaws, the teeth prowess the season of sanction,
Of locked array of madness
A malady of culture, a sleepless Lagoon of silence,
The fishes bled the dangerous, the Piranha they lay intrepid
They bite the dinner, they crave the medusa,
Of winged culture, the whaler of torrent

THE WITCH DOCTOR

He the Shaman of the tribe, the Disposer of nation hood,
The State side, the furor of Zealous,
He rasped the medicine bag, his Clover,
The who, you dare, the Hoof, Indian tattoo
They favored the marble headed Jackass,
He cried the Fires of Country, the rose he depraved,
The silver twilight, beige, the doctor of midnight
The accrue of wield, the battle axe, the snare
They proved jeopardy of Nation, the Sioux Indian
The fur giver, the drunken slather, the whiskey peddler,
They disposed the emblem of Keepsakes medallion of thirst, the tiger
The pentacle spear head, a Doctorate of blemish
The reconciled the witch, the heaven's erupted a slur of activity
The Indian walked the hot coals, he snaked,
A pittance a Pit of hive, relinquished the needle
he raised the snake, his lips barbaric
And the iron of white foxes lair,
The barbarous naïve, the ridicule of poison
He baited, he cried the spirits

THE PIRHANA

They Scathed the Amazon, the Piranha
Of Depth; they cried the oceans,
The shells of Season, they bask the wicked,
The crocodile laughed they Eat
A Devour, a Hungry they lay the Bilge

The dry the Ravenous, tide the turtle
They Destroy the under Currents lays, bitterness rules they croak
The idol, they laughed the ring tail, the Man Cries
The wind swept of rivers, the climb, the Amazon
They Shepard, they Devour, the everything,
They sty the Currents refreshed the seasons
They eat, devour the respect of the lion

THE BOWER BIRDS

They prey the antelope, they stave the marshes,
Of forests, they cry the Open wares
The rains they came wade, the hail it belts
Of pretty lay their Fur, they feather the winged canary,
They trite the wash, the mighty Ovens River they collapse,
The pretty pink tide, the clover Dry, the Violet trees, they swoop
The burden, a multicolor they perturb the twilight,
They Chirp the whicker, barrels of India, they laughed,
The oceans of paradox of tears shed unbroken midsts
Broken hearted the bower birds, their Cages bare,

THE BALD EAGLE

He raised his Head, he broke a Chick,
He Cried the Homer, he bask the ridicule
The momentous display of pride, he cried the wing tips,
The, over the clefts, he hovered the icy dew, he clamored
He stood still, motioned the cloud, he cried as the prey caught
She motioned the forget me knots, a Deer laughed
The paddocks of prairie of indecent fervor as the carrion landed
The incandescent wavering Dove, the deer Caught a feather,
The winged apparatus flew, the wavering of Talons, they Caught the deer,
The eyes sunken under, as they swooped on the prey

THE WHITE WHALE

He Crowed the Ships ballast, the master of the deep
The Old Ahab of mastery, he played he mule of incandescent,
The Violet seas, he partook, the ship's Captain, the whaler
The Dream suspense, the whalers of the deep
The narrows, the scoundrel, the Brook, the Stage

The scene is set, beset the Giant leap of the depths
Of the Green whalers gave chase, the fellows, of Crewmember stout,
The Dreams of black fellow ordained
The streets, they barged the Crook, they stowed the iron of harpoon Dread,
The spear pointed the yellow Coat of Ahab,
He stammered the bastard of whaler, my eddy of Open tides,
The Crook of yellow, the dog of the open Seas
The Portuguese man of war, mellow my rite,
The white whaler esteems the rubble, a catacomb of steely eyed vengeance
Marrows thy Wedge of embittered fools, for the doubt of fire,
The Cruel Ardent of seas of terror, they plummet,
The death of the Violet seasons I admire the skirmish of the whaler
The death of the white whale Ulysses tenacious

THE SHARK

They rasped the Underworld, the Seas blight havoc,
They Cried the Whaler, the black terror of the deep,
They Strove the Grey nurse of the Steep,
Underlying Coves, the shark bay, the isle
Of shark Cove, they Cry, the under the reefs
They patrol the depths, the shoals, the tug leapt astray,
The Santa Maria she Sea captain a Shoal
Of St Peter's Relic, the burden of Seas,
The squall, the baron seas, the hull a wallow,
The ever-present Deities of the Deep, the white pointer,
Rasped the whaler, shoaled the Caverns Deep asunder, the waves
Reamed, the tears of thanksgiving,
The impenetrate, the impending Doom they lay dormant
The sleeping whales of burden, the whales they lay still
The Dolphins their predator of narrows strait
They cry out the move, the splashing sub scene
The undercurrents flatulent glimmer, they stagger the Maria
She tugs the sublime, the skipper, of the whaler

THE ALBATROSS

He flittered the streams, he bard the even
He raved the song, oceans of Driftwood,
Scenic he groveled, the Fishes he plucked, the shed of feathers
He created a winged Prometheus, the pot belly stove, he rallied
The wingtips melted, the streamed array of virgin in flight

He Drove seas, Streams he Vegetated the oceans he billeted
The Sermon he felt, he barbarous the nephew, a Kingfisher
The rabble a tear, the swan preyed witness, he rebelled
The sport of it, he preyed a beckoning triumph
The wingtips he caught a blade of fisheries Grub,
The turtle array of diner, a pity of appreciation, the dove of aspire,
The Dou of Deer, the petty motioned to the dwarf,
The scenic rabble, the Prometheus of dragon
Fortuitous glimmer, the nightingale, pocket of air lifted

CAROLS BY CANDLELIGHT

They swarmed the palace of the Myer Music bowl
They cried the hush, the candlelight vigil, the hush settled
On that Bowl of Musical surround flurries
The Organ of Still, the pocket watch cried
They motioned the Brass, the orchestra fiddled
The prone of announce, the melody stiffens,
The twilight till dawn, they sing
The Crowds befuddle the surrounds, the sounds ornate,
The tears of the young; moonlight till dawn they play,
The Choir settles, they séance, the echo of Singers glee,
They primrose the olden time, they beckon the floral abundance,
The flora they Chorus, the night's 'arbor of Venue

THE CANDLE

The laid waxed Vigil, the romantic evenings midst
Lowly, the Candle burns softly,
The acquired tastelessness, the brim,
The wax smalls of Vicarage the Church of Bells,
Cry the smoke of Candle allows
The burden of Carols by candlelight, a slight adage
The cursory of flickered, the wax of blessings,
The fruitful stare, the flicker refreshing duo, the blight
The cool midst, of exterior, the dripping, of gently drip of waxeth dwarfs
The remiss awaits the toil, the meditation, the candle drips dry
The wax of effervescent, the candle, the wayside
Bypasses, the fusilier, the Candle
The life of Candle, littleness of specter, the light simmers,
Smallness of latitude shed the light, the flame of torches a blessed

THE GLOVE

The hand fits, the glove permits,
The sermon of dereliction of squire, kind sir!
Dear Sir, my impoverished notions, the Fast wit
I encompass thy pardon forth wit the English, the hat, the umbrella,
Naked without the glove of personable fit,
The hand baggage wept the Dear glove of knit
Coat of Chime the bell, a dear wife, a righteous of melody,
Whip the ragged he rope, the Bootstrap, the glove
O' shameful scoundrel the blight of aftershave,
The scent fore bitten the moustache of gray

THE PUPPY LOVE

The pet O' puppy, the love of hands felt,
The touch of Balwyn, the Dow Jones Cowboy
She felt her quake tiny quake of nipples, wedge
She robed his in hers, they laid a touch, they Cried
The gentle the robe of Darkness splendor
They felt, the love of generations of synthesis
Gentile, the Crime of a moment's grasp, the kiss, they clasped,
The riches of violet, a growth, the Faberge
Of Stolen romance of Dear one
Immersed the pleasure of ecstasy unraveled,
The tidy knit, gray, the tidy encroach
Preponderances wept, the growth, the tips they pledge
She bought a bottle of Crème,
He foul swooped the arcane surrender,
The shared, the intimate, the ornate tips
Desolate, they psaltery the glances,

THE WINDS OF DENMARK

The autumn winds blew, the shower of petals
The frivolous of breezes, they spelt the glimmer
The autumn wind went by, the winter yet as yet
The summer came; a dawn dew felt, the breezes, the drought
Fell, the abundance of cherries, the spring it seemed
The tide of la porch Etta, the street café
Adorn those petrified woods, dry as coats, swelter
The farms they swelter, the autumn passes away

The spring lay bouts, the abundance of leave-gray
The ought they splendor, the dusty breezes, the furrows
The flies they caught, shadows, the heat haze
The splendor of dismal, the midst of leaves
The mirage, the little desert of fauns, grays and pinks
The grandeur of dismal, the snowy and the fellows
Sat, for a cold beer, a shanty my fine barkeep
A peppered steak, for a heated sunny day
They leagues, the wine, the street café, the talk
The idol whispers, the ladies, girls of whence they came
The chatter of golden haired cockatoo snatchers
The cravings the laringo, the sheriff came to town
The tourists settled for a cheery afternoon beer
The river sighed a catch, afterwards, the bream at work
The boys went home, for a cool one under the patio

THE FEUD

The Mc Klintlock and co. a dusty old shanty
The boys they set, a sun whip, the tide had turned
The breezes set, the shutter slam shut, the autumn breezes
The spring a fine potato crop, the setting of eerie shadows
The noon day sun, it crept over the horizon
The girls Harriet, nurser, and petty grouse legged
She cried old hoarse the noose has settled the beef, extracted,
The old boy went to collect, the firewood
He belched, the axe man of the wood, he cried
Old Martha, the streets of old hard wicks timber is closed
The belly up the stove, betta collects the fresh timber
He dote the axe, he climbed aboard the chufa
He chopped that thieving' mongrel dog
A shot rung out, the man of the house was dead
He calved old Clancy; fetch the gun, the Leroy he snowed
He fetch the rope for the Elroy clan, the shots a pivotal array of sounds,
The boson caught, the bandit he stirred
He fired a round, of dummy, he shouted, got the brother
The snake caught a gypsy wood, he drove the kangaroo
He fed the old doctor; he chased old Elwood, the clam
He fed the golden retriever, shot the dog, old bustard died,
He snowed the petrified wood

THE IVORY TOWERS

A myth in the shadow, the vexation of fat cats
The heathen of old liquor brush, he fired the show pony
He wealth the doctorate, the rich mans' idol, he summer
The shotgun marriage he prepared, the bush and co
He wrote a tall effigy, the dregs of cotton, and the fine silk
He sold the house, a mortgage, he indebt the bank
Stole the riches, the coudrey of the orchard, they were to meet
The old daughter, he beset her privilege, he wed the chaperone
He gasped the pride of misers and co
He broke into tears; the old mix bought her out
He shed a penny reserve, the share holding plummeted
He said the old mix and co, bet you they fought,
They sold up shares, the ivory tales
They smoked the quarter earnings of halfpenny dollar
A strawberry, they picked, a yearly earnings of quarter a million,
The street clamored a Yorker, the workers of the hive of activity,
The marriage convened, the daughter smoked a sling shot
The cigar burnt a Cuban, the boys they starved
For a king size, a beef on the carve, the fat cat announced,
The wedlock her sister the fat cat announced
He sister sera she maiden, a martyrdom

THE HAVEN

A haven of streets, the glen of motor oil
The needle of throttles, the pistachio of chip
He remarked bourbon for the dry bitter taste
He slouched a throttle twirled, the how and where
The shudder of brakes, the climatise, a raw deal
The motor revved, the ground tumult, the eerie sly
The cotton picking brakes, the handbrake turn
A doughnut slide, turned the wheel too fast
He cornered a groove, the jug of beer, he wed
A girl, she cried Yallumba Street, Blackwood
She swerved the tiny outback town, the watsonia
The nillumbik of patriarch, a town of forefathers
Hey revved the side streets, they shimmied the tires,
The Yallumba Street Parties are us, the Blackwood of crows nest
The hornet peeved, the stereo played, the boy got drunk
Steady on! He wed a girl friend Sharon, she cried
For ray' to come, a come a cropper with the boys'

THE CROOKSHANK

The wiry old man of thirty-nine, he peddled the shine
He laughed break out of jail, he broke a tear at the slum
The matron he cried lend me a suit, a raincoat, he glimmered
The soak, he cried how you paint a beard on the dummy
He made up a salt a ceramic of himself
His clay a face, he portrayed a cloak and dagger
The scheme of things, he rabbit a dug, through a hole in the wall,
He caught the prison guardian, the warden cried
He built a nest, the birdman of Alcatraz he wept
He burden the silken necktie, he cried a flat chest,
Of hope he pulled himself, through the tunnel
He dug the sewer a glen, he sought the backwoods
He declared the pipe-line dug, he sought the fire
The Ulysses of tyrant, ran a muck, the shell-scrape
He dug, the wart hog he pleasant, the bacteria
He wooed the woman of his dreams

THE INKLING

He sailed a tall ship, a fighting vessel of nomad extremes
The oceans Atlantic, the whaler of eddies, the grim fight
The blue whale, the hunt is on!
The grimster, the sea captain, the Ahab of the relief tug
He grimaced the white whaler took my leg
He skunk the liver, the back-bone of tyrant
He fed the soup, to my tyrant son
He belch the keg of rum basket, he tread the scheme
A pocket full of tuppeny-dive, this shed nickel,
Of golden ingot be found, the finder of the grim reaper
The whaler pleas his liquor salts, the backbone
The dread of the high seas, he capitulates the poisonous,
Brew the stank of whaler he fell to his death
He drove the old man whale, he dug the ditch,
His men cried a dark-horse of whaling ships
He drove the kindred, the whaler he butte
His calamity the old vessel, he drank a pot,
Sty the old riddle, dive the sackcloth of time begot
He shimmied the turtle, he skunk the gunship Idaho,
He felt a steer, the moat for my portion, a liquor of dread
He foul stunk the dregs dry, he farewell the mess of liquor

THE COURT JUGGLER

He ran the gauntlet, the four winds of paradise inn
He stole the maiden of his dreams, he sure footed
The king he wept, a good tidings to you, have Shaw!
He laughed at the servants, they made his dreams
He crowed the effortless quagmire, he drunk a portion
He stowed a fighting vessel, the king made a tune
He saved the castle Camelot; the king made his a juggler
He laughed till he poured a poisonous brewery
He drove the jester wild, to oblivion with the vicar
An insult drove his linen basket, the gallows with the juggler
The king defamed a privilege, he tore the head
That juggler rotten egg, he sowed the head
He poised to stagger, the head rolled off the jester

THE JEHOVAS WITNESS

He wooed the doorstep; he cried the detriment of the churches
He wooed the campaign of door knocking, a foot in the door
The contempt of those Hebrew slaves! He laughed
A cloudy look alike, he wooed the boys at the pub
He crowned the silken ladies dresses, he decided to change
A tack for the ladies ribbon, a Jehovah door knock
A ladyship likes to read, our edition of holiness splendor
He favored the rheumatoid arthritis's victims
They will listen to my knock at the door
He clove a silken dummy, he fed her jeopardy,
The lady with pierced dumplings, it's a sin he cried
She woven a factual tale, he cried, a lady of the night!
He needed her forgiveness, he cried my lady
A biblical fact, a mirror of trees passes in the night
But, Jehovah witness does splendor the rights of others
We of Jehovahs witness stead the brewers nectar, the ladies have the rule

THE BOYS' OF THE RANCH

The boys' they cried the Jackaroo, he plummet
The old kelpie, the dredge he sowed the seed
The boy out on the town tonight, better esteem the mother
The old lady cooked a shank, she wallowed
The chopper flew, the cattle crossing they bemused

The emus leg race, they had, the bottom dollar for a two up game,

The sixes for the old shed, the bone the aborigines took, the white fellow

He befuddled, the old acubra hat, the stubbier shorts

The whip, they laid, a commoner jackal he drove

The drovers they defiled the coyote, the languish at arms

They drove a kangaroo, spotted that old bustard

They shed the boots, crocodile caught the old mare

Have to save, the mare, the koala bear seedy old rump

We plough the dim view, we Scottish the kelpie for a white cross

We plague the old woman for a knitted half shank

OUTBACK

The outback they fled, the settlement of paddy

They cured; they flew the nest of Absalom ranch

They Stowed the Ute, they wept the pub,

The Stories of Outback, and the history of Shirley, they told

The brewery they staved, the pub wrought a pack

Of druid, the maid asked, where's the dungaree of wipe

The old black fellow, the shearing shed of blimey,

The folk tale they basked, the drover sunk the beer of profanity wise,

He grasped that old eddies, and he spelt the liquor store backwards,

He drove the sheep, the boys climbed upon the Jeep,

They went Frog spotting for the nearest kangaroo of Dark horse range,

The dog he caught the Scallywag, a principal he fought

The boar of wild oats ate the bleeding Carcass,

He chased the hound into Submission,

He ground old salt of peter, black he peppered

The old post and they drove the Bunyip ranges,

THE OCKER

Footy-shorts, sneakers he fed the old beer

He drunk a cold stubby of ice cold bitter, he flagon

The old carnival, he raced the girls, a guy he asked

Is there a pub in town! The wag glanced sideways

He struck bullion, a girl! He added, a Sheila

He slam dunk broke the is da grizzly tycoon!

He bard the old top shelf, he hungered for a meat pie

He woke the old publican brandy, he laughed

The boys' won't shed a two up game! He stowed old fence

The rabbit proof fence to the bloody wire

A fucking' doughnut for a sweet thing such as you!
He struck a country bumpkin', he loaded the stout pickup
The Ute he proclaimed a bandana frog the Doolittle
He drove the bloody pickup, he stole the sheep
He possum spotting the rabbit fur, he kept a shear in the Utility

THE CROSSBOW

The sow of grape they splendor, the abundance of pleasure
The ripe of guns, the plague of pompous raw
The sword it bowed, struck the needle, the bone it cut
The balustrades, the ladders they fought, the juggler laughed
The riddle laughed, the jester he played a game
He fats the pillage of pork, he stowed the violent uproar
He scorned the ladyship, Guinevere, he stole her chastity
He marveled the croak the iron porous seeds of jest
He longed the toe, he crawled the bottom, he doughnut the hole,
The black empty pit, he Roth well the liquor
He marveled the old catweazle, he languor the magi
He staged a holdup, roll them up! His direct assault
A turmoil he toe the bishop, he sold the barnacle down the river of moat,
The drawbridge, the templar raged, the hornets nest he floured the chook

THE HIGH SEAS

The Christianson added a plague of two foot
The allie he plummeted, the hold he sold down river
The boys they cried a black terror of the seas
The Ahab he longed the jeopardy of lice, the mice have it!
He stabbed the coxswain, he delivered a sermon
He cried lamb of god, precious little I have perturbed
I dry up the gray horses, the draught of assault on the winds
Of no denial, the king tide has bled the rumpus plague
The delirious of pock marks, the face of blood, the brood
The white whale I ketch, the seamen erupted a tear
The rum ration he devoured, the silken cross arm splendor
The bassoon of dry dock her scabbard, the recluse of shipyards in denial,
The cross arm a diligent pear, the naked booth
My dire inability to share, the golden ingot I despair the seasons built
I wrote a book of sow crop, the needle of junket
The sails are full; the winds do harmony, apparent
The gnaw of mice among the woodless, the oak of hers

The cargo, the hold has her beech wood, the aft deck has
A world of earthly abundance, the keel haul for the locust
The hair brained fool, the treachery of bottomless pit

THE CLOUDS

The howling seas of June, the specter of silken lows
The highs they hide, and pray-tell, they seek the abundance
The growth of haven, the siblings they seek, the passage of time,
The garble of moderate winds, the thunder of clouds
The wither of Wentworth, the clouds of moderation
The silken virtueless of clouds, the acclimatize of brook
The lady-spring, the lows they do fiber, the horn of fearsome might
The splendor of cumulous, the stratus enveloped a tear
The thunder by understanding, the pencil-brook lows
Harmonies the frequency, the up-lift, the drag, the phosphor bright and yellow,
The darkness dwells, the horn of good hope

THE COUNTRYSIDE

A ladyship of parable she totters, the sleepy wallow
The cottage, the outback town of Illinois, she weds a cow syrup
She lows the buttress, the English flower garden, she appends
Nutrient, bedfellows, the badlands of the sleepy wallows
The mutter of the sheepish cat, she discreet the fernery
The children', her little begonias, she carves a leg roast
A busy, the kitchen, she awaits the pop, she lends her pet sympathies
She appeases the stolen dogwood, she frets the time of idle
A capacity of remembering, the silken necktie, the fashion of hat
The overcoat of darkened exterior motif
A hello mamma, the dinner on the slide-top table!
The fashioned old bank-house, the trees of fig, and the jam she prepared
So thoughtfully, she aligned the pear strudel, the apple of wend
She marveled the spent herbs; she cried her cauliflower and sago
She aberfaldy her Greek spotwood mule, the darling peaches are ripe

THE KNIGHT'S RYME

A Dante of eternal inferno, he wept as he resounded
The fires of hells kitchen. An ambition, quirked the knight
As he wrote a bard he cried thou knights plea

The bargain of syrup, the blend of sour
The goat's cheese, the bath he pronounced
He drove the wicked, he peddled suffitus
He wreaked a tankard of ale, the peddler sufficed
He drank of the milk, a bosom he roasted
The ladyship he delighted, the knighthood

THE HAND MAIDEN

Her dresser table, she bled, the ointment rub
Her elixir she painted, the fertile abandonment she lot
She paraded a gift horse, the mouth she caked a stick
A lip gloss, of fats of goat, she bed the oil of fox
The pixie she cried, the Deloris her maiden glory
The lady of her conclave, she called the squire
A ladyship wants a privy of eloquent, endearment!
To a troubled dwarf of Fatima, relief my sordid tale!
My disease of there is no cure, my fine ladyship!
Be sent to the sword, the squire will whip me not!
I abscond the dearest, the riches of my soul!
To her ladyships' pleasure, the gallows of rum pot pie!
I deliver the kitchen for my lord king of Alfred!
A lateness I decree, the pond I am very sore!
The mercy for the pig. the swine have it not!
I cry at the mercy begotten thee, please judge me not!
She delivered a scoundrel; instead a cow suckles at thane sweet merciful self,
I divulge of river of green, fountains, the cockles of heart I brandish the wicked
Of mischief, a mere child of convalescence means, decreed jest
My stead of worshipful mood, my vengeance shall be upon thee!

THE FIGHTING SLOOP

The Egyptian fighting sloop, a carry-on it slaved
The slavers trade, the black caught a shackle down below
The bong, bong of the drummer counted the beats
The oars paddle, the shears do stem, the pride
The silent beckoning, the slaves grovel, the stem to stern
The paddle of iron, the below decks, the haven for dead, the heathen spite
Settlers they paddled, the leprosy of ketch, the hold of iron
Foretells the grim survival, the after decks they paddled
The Egyptian met, a grand hurrah, hurrah of the whip
The Norseman of sail birds, astray, the virgins billed

The pocket of blood, brood the stout decking
The shovel of fire, to the catapult, fires from hell
The burden of the sling erupted, the cat whip of sail
The harsh pantheons of just, the Roman dictator of philanthropy
He squalled, the righteous peddler of might
Exercised the divine right, he corrected the spoils
The long boats of sleuth the peril of Poseidon
Save us all! They cried a bustard through the muck
The sneer of scabbard duel, the sewer rats down below

THE CLOWN

He ravished the stage, he cried its bozo! He doe the clown
He stole the tarax club, the laneway of channel seven
He ravaged the audience, he cried the speakers aloud
He brandished the little folk, he laughed aloud
The clown talked funny, he gloat the screen, the drawn curtains
He climbed above the clouds, he laughed and wept, he cried
He roamed the paddocks of his dreams, he stole jeopardy
He laughed the bozo is a clown, he said my goodness grandmother!
The clown stayed a prairie hat, the pom, pom astounded the boy
His clover the leaf, he cried the boys have a feat, the astounding
Free for all, a free raggedy ann. doll, he tried to stay awake

THE WIND

The whistling eaves, the eerie tormented gapes, the swallows,
Fought the winds, the preponderances, the streams of gale
The force it blew the wings fluttered, the awesome breezes,
Flung, the eerie tumultuous breezes, the birds flung
The gale it flung, the virgin skies, they prolong the agony
The entice, the whalers, caught in the breezes
The pea it wallowed in the wind, the winglets soared
The wind denied the bellowing Chinook flew backwards
The soaring bows, the bowels of thunder, the skeet it crowed
The tender midget, the virgin in flight, the winged Prometheus
The tether of Richard, the mask of facade, the falcon stormed
The patria dish, it fell a warning to those below, the awesome,
Flight of the pigeon, the strokes of thunder, the lightening pondered
The bald headed eagle swanked a bane, he stole,
The virginity of Auspray, the jitters held her

THE GOAT TRAIL

A path dwindling, the moonlight curves, the rocky bypasses
The single minded mule, he burros the dealt curve
The mountain goat fed, tree of buttress, the winding
Snaky ravine, the coarse way, the Smokey path, the mountain streams
The winding path it dwindled, twirled, a wend throughout the narrows
The parchment slipped, the goat caught a blind affidavit
The swung, he grappled the steep, the gradient spilled
The mountain pass wanted a blood-line, the prowess, the climb
The packers of dirt-water-fox, it rambled, a bread-line
It crumbled as the Richard, it moved, the gateway to hells kitchen
He crowed the mightiest ravine, the slipway of curve, and the dirty lone warrior
The picnic to lone-pine, the shadowy princes
The apocalyptic horseman, the gray rose admired
The thorn of ITA, the skeric of women's' rosary
The admirable saint, the scorn of allegro bypass

THE VALLEY OF THE KINGS

Heroes beset the graveyard, the auspices of terror
The slaves, the acute maidens of dreamt, the ladyship
Burdens, those whalers need a concoction of smite
The kings must have, the adornment, the jewels
The slaves, the second life, and the hereafter they stay
The blank notoriety, the king Horus, they stave
The gorgons, the stem of perpetuity, the order of saints
The might of the legions, the say yet spear of throw
The order of Prometheus must, can do, a séance of taboo
The royal affinity, of leprosy phantoms of green pastures
Their rule of the giants, the pyramids, the ocean of danger
The fathoms of fur givers, the seas of lost souls
The burden be upon thee, the master of Ephesus decreed it

THE TEMPLE

The pyramids of isosceles the maddening plagues,
The slaves they beheld the riches
The Dreams of the Cleopatra she moved
The earth, she wrote the plague, the grain Silos
She reaped a Serpent a hound she malice
The Stifle, she Killed her hand maiden

The dreamt of Antonio's of Arthur's the stone,
The Romany she plagued the broke
The Sons of Daughters, they hovered, the slaves
Slather the buttress of York
She sailed a sloop of Carrion, the nightingale she billed the pigeon
She fell, a Dove a love she scoured
She Scoundrel that Dreaded pink whaler,
She cried the Romans of Pompeii the Diety
Of Love, she Sloth the purple a Harriet
Of apathy, the Dreaded whaler the Sorcerer
She Dismissed the Daemon of Goad,
The servants she blight the scimitar of wealth
She Scoundrel the leper of Deep,
The hornet she plagued the wretched
Klondike, the dove slung a grape of Serpent asp
It bite her nipple, the Carrion they leap the frog,
The son she beget the Solace of Verdict;
They worshipped the dog o' Horus the lion they reaped, the lizard

THE LOYAL SERVANTS OF EGYPT

The throne of Egypt, the bethroval of heathen
They stole the slather, the marshes, and the valley of kings
The pyramid of Ulysses, the valley of shadows
The suffixes of Cronin, the king of slaves, the Greek
Prometheus rubbed the ointment, the crypt they spill
The dog of lions head, rabies, the cleanser of heathen
The herpes of scabbard road, he boasts the fetish
He basked the Ivan of terrible, they worshipped the head of lion
The idol of Alexandra, the general proofed a twain, the poise
A dose of hypocritical ointment, the potion he died
Acanthus the praetorian guard the spoils for the queen of glass
The remedy of potions she died, the asp she spoil
The Marcus the terrible, he owed the hypocrite, his tartar
The bees of incantus rub; the sacred burial applies an Egypt
The motion of dregs of iron Casket River of blood, applied
The sloops they burnt, the casket bedfellow imp, he shed a grace
A whaler they escorted, the trudge with Indies of the west
They worshipped, the goddess cat, the reproach rat, the prominent
The fine silks, the jewels, the echoing marvels, the slavers
Of black palm tree ointment, the ethics shoals luscious girl's finery
The Cleopatra of Egypt toil the roman deity, she lust
She killed the fine maiden, her dreams beckoned it

THE DUNGEONS

The eerie dungeons, the cobwebbed bunks, the stale loaves
For suppertime, the gladness remembers it, the arcane he devours
He sours the goat's milk, cheese, the rotted misfortune
He cries cell keep, get me out of here! He brims he slops
The bitterness of deepening sorrows, the wells, the gut, and the shackles cut deep
The stony eyed jailor, he stales the bread, the service with a smile
He key thrust a burden as it opened a cell door, the creak of winds
The blown of winds, icy mood, he cried, key keep stale the burden!
Seal my bones to the end of this day!
The grizzly shackles rustled, the winds, the saturated, bloody rags
The heathen remarked, a blaspheme for the jailor scorned
He laughed; I could make your find a bit more snugly! Key-keep!
The rattle of chains, the sadist of orgy, stealth of minagerie, the grub-steak
A beef extract, the slop of gruel, the bread of lice
The bucket of sewage device ploy, he stole the oatmeal!
He remarked a blade cut; the prisoner wept steel derided
The spew of reckoning, the puddle of steer stew, and the jailor reckoned

THE DUTY OF CARE

The grim grizzly, labor of love, the carers' leap, the throttle
The paraplegics neck, he stayed up late last night, he laughed
The beer of stoop, the Frigidaire, he staved, the cooler of cold ice
The beer he belated a premise, a sentence, the Dockers union
He calf, a young girl, she Philomena, the girl of his dreams
He befuddled her destiny with a shovel, the high-five on TV
His growth the hard-on, he slipped her a wink, he slather
For her love and affliction, a destiny paved in love
The steel he wept, the bitter duel at odds, the fresh she loathed
The boy of shattered dreams, he wedlock the tears, a license
The esteem she beheld, the offering to marry, the virgin of the cloth
She felt the wind, the pull of hormones crete, a Turkish by maid
She singular, the pathway of spoils, she fried a dumpling
She did a fancy swell, he bed herself, he loved her cry
They said no going over the street today! He laughed
Her dismal blessings for a bed of youth, a tidy seaman
An astray she burdened, the silver slipper

THE TRIBUNE

The praetorian guard he felt, a sword, a kilt of iron
The stand alone he wrote the king of the Jews, he drove
The pickle, he held a helmet, he killed for the sakes of it
He wooed the Christian Prometheus, he mediocrities a shower
Of bowel, he stowed aboard a tall fighting vessel
He cried the consulate general Pointus-pilate
He judged the lacquer, he whipped those slaves
The shackles drawn and quarter cried an iron, defeatist none
The gender he wrote, a dangerous of Brutus suffered
The contempt, a virgin lice-driven defeatist none
He riled the Caesar general, stand and be defeated
He Vow a Portuguese man of war, he stammered the bright
The Stay-sharp sword, the bludgeoning ointment he rubbed
The wench of gruel, the sufferance of shattered bodies
The blood of slaves I brood, I farewell thee Apollonius of tyanna
Knew none to ramble, the pig of oats I hammered once!

THE SLAVER

The pirate of the seas, the boat's captain he snuffled
He withered the tall sail, the Davey-jones-locker, the seas have it!
The boys they called the captain, a blood-brood of giants
They called the old Ahab, the old man, the resolute the tall gripper
He drank a pint of Irish blarney, he kissed the cabin boy
He cried the shackles down below, the Oscar, the pilot of boson
He laughed a wicked old man, he brandished a scimitar
The boys they scallop the Wentworth, the old rosy, keel haul
The sewer rat they scourged, the quarrel wit the skipper
Left him bone dry, the Jolly Roger flew, the stagnant seas
The Portuguese tanker, the finery of gold, the ladies ridiculed
The decks of that old barge, they fired a scabbard across the bows
The shackles of men trapped below, cried merciless traitor of league of pirates
The blacks their idol, the bong of the seas, the league of snapping, pots
The old sea captain caught the wheel; he fired another across the beam
The beam fired, a myth it settled, the starboard blown off, the reckless keel

THE HELM

The bridge she plummeted, she fell, the storm brewed
The seamen caught a rigor, a wave crashed, the helm ridiculed
A blank draught of wave, firm the old skipper, he drove the Wellington
He reaped the peak, he ripped the hull into oblivion, he hauled her stern
He stole the peak, the narrows of the reef, he capitulated the seam
The hull burst a wild horse, the lady of the bow, the sails gorged
A frequency of reap, the ocean tore her beam, a stout one
A liver of poor seamen's idol, the cataclysm caught the benefit
The ovens of seamen's whirl, the skipper held the rope
The ocean died, a burly of seaman caught the wave, the boys
They tug, the wheelhouse jittered, the haul of mast, the deciduous climb
Clamored, the beach master he welled the stout, the old boson fed her steam
The anchorage of Alaskan, the roaring forties they screamed!
The oceans head the coastline wavered, a degree of hope shimmered
The purple monstrosity she waver the head of steam
The nightingale of passage, the East Indies she fed, the typhoon spread
Her bows they laughed, the mire of open seas

THE CRYPT

The crypt her shoals, they weep, the lost soldiers cry out in disarray
The shrine, remembrance of flags of duty squalor, the heathen
He worships the fiend, the allegro of spite, the howitzer blinds
The motion of lost soldier digs, the scabbard raw with dusk
The lone pine, the diggers of old, the recluse of Shepard
The dire of dead, the dead do stem, the riot of gun nests do wallow
The evil enmity of rounds, the entanglements lay bare
The strong they suffer the dysentery, the curbed desire
The Hun machine gunners, the riddled rounds, the tuppence gender
The Turks they spy, the beaches lazy with sounds of death and dying
The needle of thrust, a bayonet pummets, the seas are wild
The deserted creaks of thunder roll the fiendish, the ploy of assault
The heathen express, the boys die, the old digger, up the bum of the lazy
Digger, the British commandeer, the commander's reap the display
Of fire power, the bayonet seeks and destroys
The undying rollover their casket bitters the toil
The blungeoning nitwick spoils a levy, as the soil, the spagnum moss spoils
The dark grey midst, purples of gunfire, the bloody rags, the mule, his donkey Simpson
He cries as the Vickers rips the hole in the shorts

THE WEAPON

A M16 Amalite, a roger-dodger GPMG M60 a hound-dog
A stick of dynamite, a c4 of gelignite, a weapon according to the army
The Australian army qualified, a corporal with a wing
A boy with a dog, a vicious hound-dog, a pet lizard, a stroke of bad luck
The f1 sub machine gun, a footy pump, a large grabber for a push bike pump
A liquor of brandivino for a wine, a grabber of bent nickel
The boys set out on the desert terrain, the fish it steal the hook
The gangland mob, an oozy machine gun, a sling rubber shot
Might course damage enough, might grab, and shoot the poor beggar
In the eye mom, got the elder of bleak passage, the army says I have promise
A promiscure elaborate fiend, he punched the buddy in the eye!
He doughnut the royal fling society with a egg and salad roll

THE TOWN SQUARE

The juggler he pierced the wire, he slung a sword, he cried St peter
He courted a young hound nickel; he cried the queen is in town!
He sprung the rat, his pet, he slung the sword shallower laughed in jest
He cried the Alfred; the king of twain has robbed a simple man of Sofia
The blessings far his wild oats, a sermon of belief, the settlement has occurred!
The Queen is off sick! She swallowed a pea, a bottomless pork sausage!
The jester ridiculed the town haler, the herald of sympathy for the town!
He basked the rites, the wizard was sent forth, Herald the boy for the Queen
Has need of your gracious Queen, the boy has founded a splendid ripe
She promenade the greetings, the town council acclaimed her spite
The nipple of her ladyship has acclaimed the virgin of the child'
The King added a spite of nonsensical dreams
The seer must be found to adequate her sickness of ills, he spoke of
The Vicar must possess great moments of obscene, the wicker
The shenanigans of a priest is of no importance, I feel the lost
The bright almighty sovereigns for the man that can steal the maiden
From destitute, deaths door, I proclaim thee tuppence, a fiber length draws
He proclaimed a knight, the town savior, he laughed the shed nickel

THE END OF THE WORLD

An apocalypse chamber fueled the fires, a depth of hungering hornets
The stem broke, the passé the engine fired, the jet flew off the ramp
The aircraft carrier wept, as the winged dragon ignited
The bomb load lose its load, the aircraft carrier, it pummet

The dwarfs of the air, the alight of load, and the nuclear ignited
The town it shammed, the light of neutrons peddled
The fright of steer, the bull buffalo they wept, a giant it stroke
The surface to air missiles fled, the bunks of the steer enveloped
A wing caught a AAA burst of cannon fire wept, the legs of pilot
He rambled the joystick., he tore the violet, the greens, the darks grays
The town of Baghdad flew, the crazy eyed hawks, the stern of bravado
The heathen of Babylon, the whore she wept, the dark eyes
The blackened streets, the crater where a gorgon once lived
The missile launched a pattern, the dark eyes, and the shattered remnants
The pillaged terror attacks, the ground forces overran the gauntlet

THE SMOKEY

The bandit raced wit the devil, he shook the turmoil
He grabbed the ocean in denial, his wedlock a melody
He shook the Transam wit a T-top, he drove the Lotus
He peddle he raced, the envelope he tore, the grim Ricardo, he tore
He faced off a daughter, he wedded the poor man, and he stole the Lincolnshire
He raced that devil, the daughter's he laughed, one-hundred kilometers per hour
He roved the bears, the old Smokey, a cagey old bumpkin, he roast
The barbecue, he toll the expressway the Port-Macquarie lane to Kansas
The straightaway he paused a remission of sentence
He staved the grill, he hit a lamp-post, and he gorged the dragon with wings
The heights he withered, the St Peter, the trident of merciless
He stole the virginity, a Dianne's daughter, he army a flout
He kidded that kiddy' car, he raced the police triumphant a melody
He wept the awesome grade; he flew into the service-station
The car launched a Weber carburetor, he roasted the attendant
The whippersnapper' owl-hoot, his grove the steer
He grave the misgivings, that peddler of the wire, a Pitt street Sydney
He kept the car, a stolen a rally-car

THE GIANT

He cried a poem, hidden away he wrote, a quatrain he laughed
He wrote the wars, the Hitler, he vibrant the Charisma, the 1812 Overture
He played palsy, he wept, he laughed the bomb, he cried
The fifteen year war, the Arab of black, he trivialized, the odd fellow
He cried the pigs with eyes, he crowed the hornets, the axe man of the wood
His growth a partisan, the woodsman of the Outback, he plundered
The welsh hornets nest, he fed a tuppence, he black the whore of Babylon

He does the paradox of nerve, the ailment, he stood the Napoleon of black
The giants of future theorem, he blended, the End of the World
He cried the odd bloke, the Mob of Triad, he does pride, The Battle of Britain
He laughed of Mussolini, the odd bloke, fired a primrose,
The pomegranate his reason for living, the Nazi hauls,
The plunder and loot, the gold ingots of mine Camp, he stole the fear
Away! he pause a river of dreams, he squire The Duke of Wellington
He gathered a moss has no reeds, he cried the Norman Invasion of Prussia
He steed the elephant, the King of Alfredo, the Alexandra the Great
Greatness follows mine! I have not succession the league of giants!

THE EXPERIMENT

They developed the bomb, The Manhattan Project, the livelihood,
Of the Brothers in Arms, the stood fast, the grenade blew
The Plutonium they splendor, the lead-pipe they burdened
They poisoned the lakes of Germany, the 235 DDT, and the strongman
The hope of ending the War, the Germans, the Allies, they demanded
They whiff, the unreason, the ripe bundle, I ketch, the valleys
A Einstein he marveled, the E=MC2 he gave the Ike, he led the betrayal
He fled the Empire, The League of Planets, and The United Nations
The Paper Tiger they portrayed, a gender they suffered from a visiting Orbiter
A Space the Nuclear Physicist he adorned the Strombium 245D
He laughed poison the dam, the Germans have a cause
The case book for the United Nations Portfolio, he lent, The Manhattan Project
Had its name, he befriended a Nuclear Scientist, he cowered his into oblivion
He struck a bargain, his fellowship, The Eagle, the primeval Dwarf of flight
They blew the Nagasaki bomb perished thousands of people
A man holding a gun etched the wall, he disintegrated, and he followed a chapter
He fell to his death, the Emperor he firm the rights, the scabbard bare its fruit
The victorious allies demanded none, they fed

THE BYZANTIUM EFFECT

They shattered the toil, a space time, the winged chariot
A helio of chapter into the book, a timelessness of grape
A Bacchus of fermentus Rubicon of space, they used a brain
A molecular rhythm, the chop of tetrahedron based
The pentagram soaked, a methodology of space, the crime he fermented
They flew about the sun, the treacherous star, the Jupiter has rings
They revealed the rings of Saturn, the gentiles they whispered
A gentile laughed, the psychic phenomena he gladdened a realm of thrust

The wire he flew, he saturated the envelope, and he drove the winged Prometheus
The dragon flew up through the chamber, incinerated the myth
The Orion he flew, the onyx he ridiculed, the Jakin he laughed
The gentiles knew a rheumatism, a gent to Largent' the appeal
The planets they skimmed, the stratosphere they plummet
The missile flew a pocket grenade, a winged star duster, the chariot flew
The envelope staggered, the chariot developed, the star-chamber drew
A blade of neutron shimmered the pane of light, the oceans bled
Her monument discovered the chambers of death

THE HAMLET OF PEACE

He cried a maiden to sleep, the Juliet he suffered an ordeal
He father an imp, he gloated the spectacle, he raved the father
He cried may I beseech thy maiden bewitched in glory
The pandemonium he believed not, the father disclaimed the virtue
He cried the stem of cutlass bride, he fermented the ordeal
He robed the situs, he clamored her seek, her hide of Venice
He ordeal the throaty Midas of castle druid, he drunken the steal
He cried dearest Juliet, myself of Mac Beth I lay privy dear Excellency
I find thou art my sarcophagus of plenty on virgin wings of pride
My dearest Judas I profound the mice of her strawberry pot
I allow my Proserpine of ludicrous my plenty, bargain thy rope
Mac Beth I steal the foil who beckons me not, they paradox my illicitness virtue
Thy sorrow of blend incompleteness, profound thy arrow, I drunkest
Oh frankness delves the wand that carries her, pomp I divulge
The treasures of her derisory cause, I accomplice they situs to perjure thyself
I laughed on golden wings of flown, thy spectacle given, ravenous
The rake it seals thy protagonist virtue on life, I must take the poison
That seals thy destiny ravel, my Juliet has depraved as such, the golden wings
She besets the seal, thou bow not, dear situs of golden, and the calf steadies not!
The Mac Beth I pioneer not, the stolen crime her father defeatist none!
He arouses fear not within mine, great solace, I amend thee punctual rhythm

THE CROP DUSTER

He flew the crop duster the virgin skies, they pummet, the clearing blues
The harsh of reds, the crops they fertile abundance,
The measure a steely whip, the joystick shudders, the plane gives lift
The oily rudder subterfuge, the hollow, the vegetable crops
They flow past; the idol winds give lift, astray the fields wind swept

The plane hovers, a momentary guise, the 245D it shimmers
The leaves of gray, the orchid they busy the fields, the dusty cropper
The seed it parasite the edges, the tinges of green, the fluttering wings
The wildlife it gorges, the scene he erupts a verse, the night sky it belongs
A cool of wind swept night skies, like the back-drop of curtains
The disarray, as Hamlet once said the cool scenes in a never-ending play
The herpes of signoras, the fluttering skirts, the tomfoolery, the scatter
The prolonged agony, entice the Richards of nurse, the nourish of cool
Spasmodiem, my like hart, the burden

THE SKI-BOAT

The ski-boat rambles, the edge of beyond, the V8 supercharged barge
The life-buoy he charges, the stem of the whip of the outboard it stems
The prairie of the wasteland, gathers the deep prolongs
The oily smell of gasoline, the gathering entice, the stern burrows under
The stem a tide, awakens the porous dusk, the roar of engines burst into life
The other boats seem prejudiced, by the howl of engines, the stem of keel
It erupts a verse, the sight of the lighthouse on dim prairie lade
Victorious, the liquor as the boy's drink, the barge it torments
The throttle belches, the squirm it tidal the wake, the bow-wave torrents
The plug it leaks, the skipper he rallies, the firm of grip, the stern bellows
The tide of king, it plummets the handle, propeller-shaft it wobbles
The deep-V hull it torments, the torn after-deck
The leaky tube, the stern it ridicules, the blustered boat, it scoured

THE SHIRILEE

He packed a dog, a pack and a scalp, a Matilda he wept, the ladyship
He peered a sing-a-long, a Acubra Hat, he dearly beloved
The score he settled, a boy in the saloon, he scotch a town whore
He stole the virginity, a lady he swelled, she cried the boy a beg nor little
He stole the rucksack, his boyhood a charm
For the road ahead, he, the boy, they met a whorehouse, the maiden cried
The boys' about town, took the sheep into their care
The road left the boys' he soldiered a barkeep, he stood high and mighty
He fried a cook, a dog he saddled, the pet poodle

THE BOHEMIAN RHAPSODY WALTZ

A song of tune, her ladyship's empire, the swan of Tchaikovsky
The froze a quire he marveled a dwarf, he swung Orchestra
He cried the waltz, her gender abhorred, the gents a liquor
The Ralph rallied to the aid, he swan her lily, he marveled the streak
The corset of Her Ladyship, the quarry swept her off her feet
The league ladies truffle, the lawyer a man of distinct amiable pledge
He swallowed the knife, the cutting edge, he cried may I
He took the dance, the finery, he spelt, and he took her off her feet
The blossom he feet, her shoes he polished, a wedlock to marvel
The quire played, a Mozart's 6th, the quarry played, a synthesis of gender
Remembered, the noteworthy father, he laughed the bride
An attaché she queried, he stole her virginity, with a two step dance
A paradise my love, eloquence is beneath thee, I follow

THE AIRCRAFT CARRIER

The nations evaded a firefight, the scourge of gorillas, in the midst of tears
The flag bearer waves the aircraft aside, the winged hornet strayed
The blue falcon, the wings of uproar, the sturdy cradle, the subterfuge
The blemish of wings, the bright orange, blues and grays,
The hornet set her prey, the gigantuous of wavered flags the gripper, the bomb is loaded
The tomahawk is launched, the parade as the skipper leaves
The destroyer of lands, the bright jolly-roger he plumes ahead
The tail section, the rudder splays, the thunder of uproar

THE SCIMITAR

The blade of the scimitar, the cutlass, the eddy of stem, the handle grasps
The blade of kings, the hurtle of the edge, the bone it cut, tore
The heathen of gypsy, he ran the blade through, he cornered the Shepard
The blank through a grip, he pried the grip, he caught the blade
A scimitar of desert terrain, the dunes of blood, sweat and tears

THE REVOLT

The Warsaw pact, a Jewish revival, the Nazis held that they would steal
The life-blood, the Jewish outbreak, of World-War-Two, the Jews rebelled
The captors, the spirit of the non-believers, the antics of the Nazi captors
The Adolph decreed they should, but should not, the disbelievers rallied

The support of Wilhelm Schmidt, he conquered, the outbreak of hostilities
He showed the Nazi leaders, he created, the Nazi movement, he welled
The shooters plagued, the corrupt they ran for cover, the Sten gun whipped
The panzer divisions they absconder, the terror beseeched those beneath
Themselves they found a brigade, the Jewish they cheated, the destitute
They delivered, the captors a pudding, a Molotov cocktail, the spirits

THE REVENGE OF SETTLERS

They sunk a ball and Minnie, the musket they fed
The Hawkins rifle they filled, the Jim Bowie he died
The Alamo he improvised, a fashion of cow-belly
The mule he cried a musket of home spun remedy
He shouldered, a pea ball in the round, the guts of it turtled
The Billy he cried, the Mexicans rebelled, the cloth of rank
The Santa Anna bled the settlers dry, he rebuked a Satisfield
He mastered the cry, the Tennessee Rifles, they monk a fashion
A fast one they drove the wedge, the yellow gold, the gleaming steel
They pitied the poor monk; the Texicans billed poor old fast Eddie
He proofed the whiskey barrel; the keg blew an honorary slave

THE KITTEN

A fur ball patterns, the kitten delves, the young princely, curly tops
The cat of wonder, it purrs, the scratch a dimple of mom, the suckling
The kisses as sweet as rum, the catch it survives, a fall of broken promises
The hairy dope ball, the hatchling from mother's own, the jump a ball
A fluff of cotton, the furry of grim, the dog chases, the little cobwebbed mace
The marshland of beauty frolics, the playful yelp, a nip of the feather duster
Entourages of fears, the fascination, the person wonder, the shriek, the kitchen sink
A drowning, the cloth, dwindling feather duster, the rascal of playthings
The enthrall of the footsteps, mother has thrown, a chosen pathway

IT'S EASY TO REMEMBER

A séance of peregrine falcon, a mother watches over, the children'
The sparkle as the fireplace burns, the crackle as the embers flown
As high as the ceiling, the joists, the cockle of wooden creaks
The remembrance gladdens, the children' wrestle for control
A Christmas fire, a day of reckoning, the Santa Claus would be climbing
The wooden of Cherrie-top, the blessings, the socks above the fire

The sizzling ham steak, and pineapple, the roast a delight, a fire burns
Softly the wooden it smothers, the ember fly, crease the golden flown
The evident of Christmas carols, the sign above the fire, the crackle of waffle-irons
The marshmallows roasted, golden and pure, as is the thoughts
The loving memory gladdens, the sarcophagus of entrée

MELANCHOLY ARVAY

A saint lays await, the church of most holy, the monastery
The lady in waiting, the glamour Percival, the priest
He cries, the nun, his lady in wait, he proclaims, a holy art thou
The bliss, the throne of Christendom, the man enters, the afternoon gladdens
The sphere of holy, the epicenter of the quire, he three develops
The quire the all-boys-school, the shiny web, the silken garments

REMEMBER ME!

The man he walks, the street-wise he commits, a unceremonious greet
The lady of his dreams, the cloud-nine, he rivets the attention
The girl looks-on, she weathers her brow, and she greets the grin
A smirk cries-out, the suffering toadstool, the etheric gender of grief

THE GHOST RIDER

The scarlet web, the symphony cried, he rode the crow cried
The pimpernel cried the loss of winged garb
The torment, the British chased, the cock-sparrow raved
The empress of sadly state of affair, the republican hid
The bandit stayed the night, the rosy the bar waitress mated
The colonial of wild horses, the stable he hung, his saddle
He farewell the rigors, a night's work, the guns, the hat
The scarlet cape, no-brother knew too well, the hope
He cried the eagle of sovereignty, the hotel he stooped
He opened the door, the favorite Inn, he horseman the well
The glad tidings, the kinsmen bellowed, the sympathetic glimmer
The British raved, the Casanova of bow, he stole the virginity

THE CATS

An opera of cats, the musical entirety, the wolves do prey
The audience stood spell-bound, the pact, a cheer, a packed audience
The dancers frolic's, the dancers they played, the cats
The scenic abundance, the fowl, a ballerina, scorches the earth
The beacon of constabulary rhythm, the stage of morsel wept
The array of cats, the dresses, the sport age, and the finery of ribbons cut
The brandishes of black, the grays, the fine linen, the girls of regression
A bleak, a pause in remission, the dancers meow, a meow
For a neat, a perusal of an opera of sound, the cats of dancers glee
They played the cat over the fiend, of mouser, the meow
The phantom of the gaiety, the stroke
The profound, delectable of appetite they drove
The signoras, the women folk hounded,
A tale of hounds, the fiendish array, of starlit perform
The ravishing of fornicate, the tigress in doubt,
The precedence of fowl they collided a Debut
With the starring Cameo, he Debut the accord,
The dancers of feline they mustered the bleak
The unseasoned of extraordinaire, the tails they whipped,
They meow the starlit, the limelight, the chorus played
They staggered the stage, an apparition of noteworthy
The scholar they whipped the stray cats

THE CORONATION

The gown of coronation a queen due, for the welsh pride,
The duke of Canterbury, the arch deacon of Wellford
The castle remarks a dove skirts, the hybrid of castle,
The stringy bark chorus of Clementine, the silken gowns
Of red and crimson, the beige setting grief, beset the crown
The jewels they constituent of roses, they cry out
The pearls of ladyship smiles, the bridesmaid she tuft a yellow hurtled
They settled, the impoverished of great one
The Spencer bride, the immense floral of expunge,
The character of myth, they beg
The stony eyed bishop, a judge of the deacon,
A discreet patron of the arts, a prolific bundle
A wise old chariot abundance of purple robes,
The children's mare they frolic the pardon of grace
The gratified dungeons the old castle, the remark of Castile

Of Benedictine of saints cry a chorus,
The Antoinette of painted stares,
They burden the shapes
The mosaics of Edinburgh Castile,

THE CHARM

Her charm succeeded none, she cowered the smile
A greeting perturbed, her gracious greeting
She methodical a spouse, a method she had not long to meet
She bothered none; she cried I have not the spouse
The motion her ladyship, he handmaiden her charisma
She cried but misses I shant know! I talent the dear, frog!
I feel but the knowledge! I found the sweet nectar of poison!

THE BIRD

The swift a bird of prey, the wings fluttered, the cape
He adorned, the grave misgivings, the turtle necked frilly
He surmounted agaves, a torn gape, and the Icelandic virtue
The wings flutter, the wind blown, the frilly neck Prometheus
The glamour a pause in remission, the fighting the tides
The gander, the goose he welled with tears, he cried
A silver stemmed, hornet bottle-brush, he resolute the becoming
The stem of sure footed, he relinquished the lot
His bravado the nest, the hatchlings, he fed the caw
He stony eyed grasshopper, a catch, a firm detail
The sure mount, the head of the chic, the motion of steel grip
The tweet suffered, the ordeal he suffered, the pangs
Of discreet, the enemy hovered overhead, the raven of falcons crest

THE DIARIES OF MARTHA

The diary of Anne-frank, she devoured, the cause she developed
The snide of accrual, the Penn brook smiles, the sate, of crook
The steer of firm breasted, the ladyship consul, the shops
She walked, a sweet promenade, a blessing of austere, conduct
Found her discreet, the attaché, a wooden stick, a mixed blessing
A crock on the boil at home must carry the burden
The stool has a leak, the periwinkle of sherry, the delight
The three children' spent half a nickel, the delight, the bubbly dwarf

The pudding has a polite blessing, the apricot plum pudding
The ladies lounge, the herbal tea, the stroke of evening
The hurried glances, the footsteps grew a pathway to heaven

THE MOTHER

She wrote a bard of English, the playwright
She dreamt, a walk down the memory-lane
The larceny spelt her horrific blend
A covert coffee, a chicory, lime and lemon essence
The syrup boasts of pleasantries, the ladies lounge of courtship
The deflower the one I love, the sketch across the botham
The explicit detail, the big smoke I must shop, the finicky
Ladyships' quarrel, the shops were closed

THE PRIZE FIGHTER

He prolonged the agony, the ecstasy he gathered
He drove the spotter, the kangaroo league of shooters
He laughed, the diligent pear, the fruit
His jungle the awareness of kakodoo, the rain forest
His Rivers lade a waist, the glen, the furphy he mock turtle
The Matilda he swamped the billabong, he settled
He cried the boys, the pub for the night
A crawl to the Aussie saloon bar
The hare, he jumped-up, he scowled, the boy is in town
He crew a fight, the boy he spat, the woman of his dreams
He threw a right-one, he jabbed, and he called the guy out
A fight for the scab who plastered the effortless
The down he fell, he worshipped the deck
He threw the terrorist out, he called the saloon keeper
A dog of seven worries, he cried blackard snipe
The bob gnat he sniper, a drunkard hit
The pie eyed old Mexican drove the drover out
He swung a bat, he cried you bustard, I'll pepper your salute
With a sad rump, he ate the porterhouse, he pig the redoubt

THE FOIL

A foil is slashed, a pivot on-guard! The sword it mires
The slash! A Columbus he reckless a denial
He purses the snuff, he allows a wreak of blood
Spattered the foil! The rebuke he martyrs, the hare
He leaps asunder, he belches the herbal, and he sows
A seed of impregnation, the death of another, the guard
He defends the prize, a foil to the gut, a wrench he cries out!

THE PUB

The squalor of Pete and the gang, going to the pub tonight!
They pilled an ostrich to a lowly gum
They bet the G G's they drunkard the pot,
A Schooner lay dead, the boys of brothel they paid a sixpenny
For the fights, they argued a fist caught, a old digger
He punched the kid out, the ramrod he caved the jaw,
He staved the gripper, the Dundee
The Crocodile man from kakodoo
He laughed, the boys, they flatly denied the 10 o'clock closing,
They fought the griping old needy
They paged the missy, they broke the afternoon
Till dawn, the coppers arrived locked out the shearers backbone
In the ok saloon the watchful of toil,
The blockhouse gorge, they flew the coup

THE SANTA MARIA

The tall sails, wind blown, alfresco! the whalers call
The dinner in the old tub, the fireman flee, the boson
Shouted! None's aware the havoc, the discipline mongrel!
Of stead I corrupt thy French kisses, the wine off needle
The point of argument, you fierce some magnates of high seas!
The thunder, rattled, the gorgons cried out, the old man whaler
He jeopardized, the sailor caught a hambone, the boys'
They hauled the keel flamboyant, the losing, long and suffering!
She's a bag of rattles, the seamen's hope chest, and the typhoon
Will not have her! The iceberg of titanic despises he rumor

THE DECKS

She blew the tides of change, the rage of hornet,
The plague ripped her decks,
He espouse she belonged, the black plague,
The sailors reaped a havoc, the island she river
The mice, the charlatan of feather passage, quakes the weathered decks
She strengthened her voyage, the Bermuda straights
She cried, the ghost ship she paddled,
And the sailors founded her decking
The channel of Saragossa strait,
She broke a sail; she whipped the main style,
A dream of gorgons arisen, the stave, the blight of her kangaroo seas
They vortex a notion, the rift of volcanic
The reservoirs of time, they capitulated the stern,
The storm of black 'arbor straits,
The Golan straits the sailors wept,
They stole her virginity, they wild the torrent, blasé

NATASHA THE ROMANIAN

A Natasha she cried a splendor, the terms of endearment
She wept the song, the marriage born of tears
She skeptical, the police sergeant at arms, the seed
The peripheral magnet, she exclaimed, I have four children!
My doe is of especially, the larger one of the two!
I taught the children, love them oh so graciously!
They have a concurrent loathing, the spectacle given!
The steer I have learned, the wasteland dear old Giuseppe!
He cried, when I escaped, the ration card fixed!
The bayonet, the guard bought me home, the Russian!

THE ROSEBUD

A floral pot, a bud-bush, a candy, lemon, lantana of growth
The Hibernian, the seed, rose-bud offers, an estranged petal
A rose envelopes a gardenia, develops, a swollen stem cries
Help me not! The stem of barbed, the frost I enlarge!
The silken virtue for a fair maiden, to spike the lovers grasp!
The rapunzal of pride, the leprechaun's name spelt backwards
For the dwarf, the fruit of stem, the dressing table drawer
The spike of the first-born, the apla do wat, the tree spoke

Of many a fine dwarf, the petals bloomed, a passage north
The stow oh how I wonder if she will pick, the exploding myth!
The virtuoso of gladdened, the prickly pear, the ripe of despair
Oh the fronds of merciless fiber, the length of tarnish!
The dwarf does it well, come too collect my babe!
The floral pot, the bud, a rose petal leaps to the rescue, a bud struggles to hatch,
The impregnation of a youthful fruit, a floral nightingale
A poplar of root, the grub of merciless tradition,
A wise old bud, the snipped of secateurs, they bulb the dressing,
The primal of doe, the grasp of flower

THE MELODY OF MARPLE

A Misses Maple of sympathies pleasure, she drove her
The little sport, the dog she walked, the corner store
The Melville and bell, the street's corner, she wept
Her little friend, her five year old, acquaintance, her belvedere
Her soldier she cried, how he lent on him, her beautiful strides
Of kind requited ways, she State Savings Bank of eloquence
My son of quarter master, the wage, a pound, sixpence
A dollar of bushel, for a colonel of tea, the sun baked corn
The elder of spokes field church, smidgens for a purple cloth
A tea-towel for the supper tonight, a tin of chicory essence
A fine delight of cherry-blossom, a fine red for pop
A delightful rosebush he Farris, the old woman will love the florist
The backyard for the idol bishop, he talked, a cuddle
The ladies have their church, the violets, and the sago pudding
A lovely state of affairs, I could! A familiarity of Freddy!
Blasted hound! He stood me up! He cheesed the smidgens!
The womanizer he pledged, the cookery on the table yet!

THE BRUCE

The Clansmen dealt a severe blow, the whopping great hammers
The rakes, they spilt the blood, the gangrenous wounds
The resolute tactics, the needle through the eye, the pencil brook,
Clans red with fear, they indulged the grape of horror
The kilt they showed, the fearsome blight, bearded knight
He bestowed the grimace, the wars wit the bloody British
The heathen ran, the Tommies through, the sword of tempo
The swill they drank, the poor clansmen, dead on the table
The British curtailed, the yellow sword, the bayonet, the cutlass

The scimitar, the rake, they raped the women folk, they killed
The villagers, they stroke past, the highland shears, stood the test
The beckon of swift, the charge of the barbarians, the prowess
Their might flustered, a conscience, a martyrdom of tall swords
The brandishing-irons they tore, the silken kilts, the dead
Do repose a smile of guile, the smith he flagon a pot
A stagger as the head came off, the Wentworth fusiliers
The stagger of blind men, the patch they caught a riddle
A Jack he plummeted, he through a horse, he spud a rod
He choked the tall sword, the cutlass he died
They charged, the Light Horse Banded, the horsemen cheered
We showed our kilts, the circumspect, and the odds against
The lily whites, the frog he caught a belly, he toad the brit
The British stowed, the muskets fired, the hamlet of Bruce staggered
A pea shot a ball, the hammer hit a clansman on the head
He cried bloody boson Amos! He guild my thresher
He Scots the tempo of grace, the ladyship won't like!
He built the paddock, the green fertile fields, and the showmanship
The valleys they brook, the fight they bestowed, the beastly contract
The British overflowed, the his nor cow, the biggest clan died

THE HONEY GROVE

The grove of floral, the flowers of orchid
They grope they pluck the rivers of trees
They beautify, the singular path, the round of apricots
Grove, they blemish the patter of rain drops,
They shimmer adultery they gradual the founder,
The grape oh the patterns of olive, the love, the incandescent floral
They bask in the sunlight ripens, the furor of bleached fruit, the ovens
The woeful the sight, the pageantry of betwixt

THE CHERRY BLOSSOM

A founder of blessings, the cherry blossom, the flowers, a strangely
Wiry old blossom, the tree of speckled a floral pardon
Of Greek, the pardon oh the sweet abundance
Of whites and pinks, buds of autumn, florescence buds, they ripen
The bees they impregnate the blue satires
The honeysuckle hues, they starlight
The buds of commoner, the hyphen of plant, it largely I personify
The tarnish, the quatrain it fellowships, the tarnish

It befuddles the wire of strangulation he wipes
The porous dusk, the plant of glimmer of fashion
It follows the bonsai of floral,
The breach of the stump it befuddles the ripe
Of blight, the buds they do shimmer
Impregnated salts the lavish, the motion it sways,

THE GREAT OCEAN ROAD

A river of tourist plague, a rooster of foregone adage
The fathers of the sea, the docile of Aires inlet
A wasteland of trivia, monuments to the desolate,
The frogs of the deep, the ritual, the maze
Of speckled, the halls gap, of dead seamen's inlet,
A blush of heathen, the terror of the high seas,
The deep of frozen aqueduct over treasure, the disgrace
Of oven's of deep sea, they trollop the scurry the waves do fend
The violent of boiling seas, the violet haze of borne, acrid dismal
Towns the frolic open days, the blow hole of destiny,

THE SEASIDE LORNE

A sleepy seaside town of Lorne, a settlers point
A Apollo Bay, of resort, a sydenham of point
The lost sailors bereaved the township
The winds of mire, the salute to lost shipping
A wreckage of tugs, the steamer well rehearsed
A hall of glad tidings, the stream of tears, and the skipper bought
The wretched foul, the catacombs of burial, sink those heathen
Bury the scourge, the shipping channels, the well dug, the blow hole
The belch of the tired old skipper, the shoals of St peter
He decks slipped the tide of reverence, the idol sails, and her whimper
The wood it slaved, the king tide it wrestles, the damned do ponder
The high tide, the blackened faces, the ladies, the despair

THE ROMANUS BASTION

The old pomp, the General of the establishment, the crows-foot
He broke with contempt, he stoolie the white, he murdered
The Jew he wept, the Corinth' he stole the virgin of the child'
He met a dark fiend, he sprouted, the Jewish of settler

The havoc I cause is inevitable he gross the Spartan

The Jonathon he cursed, a proud scholar, he nursed

The wicked he accused, a heresy he proclaimed

The Jew he crucified, he crust the bread, he stood in contempt

He doesn't do for a slave, his standing doesn't concede!

He rebuked the Herald, the Clamour-boy, he escorted

To the hangman's noose, quarter and bone the mustard!

He shimmer's the flat, the skirt of those flirt!

THE GUARD

The Brigand of the colonel, he dried a foot-servant

He barged the side-of-a-door, he stole the Jewish ideal

He reprimanded the settlers, he showed, the peasant

He barbarity the Clydesdale, he defunct the avid

He revealed the inch worth, he stole the temple away

He fashioned a noose, he crucified the Jewish

He stole the avid; he cried neck the silly bludgeoned idiot

The Pontius Pilate, the Governor he wretched the Santos

He basked the Brabacus, the cure, he wretched the mule

He took a wine into the place, a prayer and a dime

A ingot he despised, he fornicated, the temple

He crazed the violet shear, he stood before the Governor

He showed the Roman Consul

THE DEVIL'S ISLAND

The convicts bred, the whalers of the settlement, Port Arthur he came

The convicts, led a stray ball, the Minnie of musket, the bled

The suffering midget, the hounds, the dogs scurried, the British

The Red-Coats they builder a Chapel, the oceans of prisoners

The pioneers run-a-muck, they escaped, captured, the capitulated

The desert terrain, the Devil's Island they sent, the evil tyrant

The lade a waist, the waistland pioneers, they swamp the backbone

Of sheep, they cried the marsh, the graze of whip, the cat-of-nine-tails

The wince of the green devils! the motion the eerie spot on the badgers back

The pink spots, the bloody, the horrendous they gather, a glimmer

The oceans of blood, they poured-out, the sympathetic bled-dry

The poor old convict, the settlement Array, Array, the scour

The red bleed wit horror, the town's folk, grimed the poor old dollar

The heathen rascals shall have their find, away boys', away!

.